WISE GUY...
And other micro fables

CONTENTS:

WISE GUY

+

4 x4

Armchair Counsellor

As If

Before and After Now

Close of Play

Euro Paean

Flamed@dot.con

Getting to Yes

Long time, a week

Love the Language

Missing Inaction

Nice Move

Remote

Smirk

Soft Machine

Squaring the Circle

The Greatest Hit

Unrequited

Untitled by Anon (*or Quite an Ado about Nothing*)

Up and Down

Winters Tales, 2

Your Rubbish

ISBN: 978-0-9558519-0-2

John F King

2009

For A

WISE GUY…

J F T King

" The original you is there from the start.
From the start you can begin."

GUY BRIDGES: <u>A Different Change</u>

I

1

' It's not for me, it's for my sister. She said you changed her life.'
Guy smiled. They often said this. He scrawled something indecipherable inside the front cover ending with the flourish "with love, Guy."
Who would question him? It was true. He did change people's lives. And for the better, even if he made things worse first. The woman holding the book looked at him. He held her gaze until she looked away first. Trick of the trade. The queue moved forward one pace. One woman left, another stepped forward. Was he a womaniser? He asked himself this constantly, particularly late at night in yet another Malmaison or – horrors – Sheraton. Guy looked around quickly. Waterstones, Leeds (well, it was Wednesday). He'd just done the usual. Half hour routine, introduction, anecdotes, question and answer, book signing.

Guy Bridges' latest book, A Different Change was top of the Sunday Times non-fiction bestseller list. That was where he had designed it to be. His publisher had taken on a US agent, the demand for Guy was so high. Although success had not come quickly to Guy it was what he put out for, planned, foresaw.
He looked at the snaking queue, going as far back as the Deightons and Forsyths in the adjacent thriller section and asked himself again: 'was he a womaniser?'
Did it matter ? Had he known these signings would be attended by 80% plus women?

' It's not for me, it's for my sister,' said the woman in blue.

' And what would your sister like me to inscribe?'

' Malmaison, room 208.'

' Malmaison, room 208.'

2

Funky first heard the news on his car radio. His top of the range – as if it would be middle – BMW was cruising over Putney Bridge.

'Radio Four Book Panel now comes to the category of non-fiction book of the year.

It's a close one in a crowded field but the winner is… Guy Bridges. You could say he's won by a shoulder, given how many listeners have emailed in saying how they feel Guy is a personal friend they can call on, a friendly shoulder to lean on.'

' Nice-ish one, Guy,' muttered Funky retuning to his more natural habitat, Kiss FM. The only thing he detested more than Radio 4 was Guy. Funky underneath wasn't really all that pleasant. He wouldn't really mind that much if Guy, for some unspecified reason, ceased to exist. Of course he wasn't utterly evil. He'd prefer the death, the advent of Guy's unexistence, to be quick. Apart from that he wasn't bothered. Accident, disease, hit squad, whatever. The image Funky carried beneath his permanently worn Kangol beret was of he and Guy locked together like two fighter pilots. White scarfed dandies, mutual respect but out to kill. Their war was about markets. Their trenches: TV studios, book launches, best seller lists.
Few people could remember Funky's real name, Funky included. He acquired the nomenclature in his first and only year at Saint Martin's Central. How and why he got to Saint Martin's in the first place was also lost in time. Effortlessly hip, he was always at the centre of fashionable circles with a Bowie-esque knack of killing off a scene at its height before waking up next lunchtime at the centre of a new one. Effortlessly.

Guy worked so hard, always had. Circuits need to be massaged. His specialism, double-handed handshakes that stopped a split second short of obsequy, eye contact held that extra second of controlled danger. Whereas for Funky it all came to him. The expression laid-back seemed too frenetic for Funky. But being second to Guy in the bestseller lists really got to him. He reached for the car phone:

' Guy, it's Funky, let me be the first to congratulate you…' He began speaking into Guy's voice mail with more grit between his teeth than was on the bridge. Although of course you'd never have guessed. Weren't they both really in the same business: self help, personal development, no egos. Who could come second in a win-win world?

3

208 was a number Guy would always remember. It had a resonance with Guy Bridges, 49. Radio Luxembourg 208. Late at night in the semi, the discernable beginnings of what we now know as rock. He reflected on how far he'd travelled, his quasi rock star life now. A city at night, his gigs- book launches so big he needed a crew of roadies to rig them up, luxury, samey hotels that made you behave out of character. Where is home now, Guy, he asked himself? He continually asked himself questions, in the way a psychotherapist is continually under supervision. Was he a womaniser, where was home, was he vain, was he on the path? The ceaseless analysis he had unleashed, never arriving. With a start Guy realised he was actually from Leeds. He'd been in Leeds all day. First class first train up from Kings Cross. Lunch at Harvey Nicks with his publisher and North UK agent, checked into his hotel then onto Waterstones. How could he have been in Leeds so long without realising it was his hometown? Was he liberated or rootless? Of course parts of the old place had changed so much since his time there. But he acknowledged his emotion in his journal: shock. He'd forgotten about his hometown.

Guy watched his hand move towards the door. The number 208 glinted on the door like a holograph. He realised he hadn't analysed why he had come there. After one knock the door was open and Guy was inside the room. Guy was almost alarmed at how calm he felt, how naturally the words and movements came to him. The woman in blue was still in blue. Guy realised how important colours were, how much the blue embraced him. At Waterstones she was wearing blue shoes, black stockings, a blue woollen skirt, over the knee, light blue cotton blouse with white bra visible beneath, blue beads. Now she was wearing the same, the top three blouse buttons open, a bra strap almost visible.

' I'll be with you in a minute, just changing. Too much blue.'
She moved confidently, there wasn't a charge of imminent sex. She was changing not stripping. In a gliding movement the woman slipped behind a screen and remerged in a cashmere cardigan. White.
After a minor raid on the minibar the woman and Guy sat opposite each other, sensible, business-like. Guy checked his reactions. Disappointment, relief? Can you feel both at the same time? It was a business meeting, called unorthodoxly may be. But certainly called, with chair and agenda.

' Maz,' she said.' People call me Maz.'

' People call you Maz, is that different to what you call yourself?'

' Jasminder Khalm. Real name. Jaz, confuses people, and I hate Jazz, except for Miles of course.'

' Miles Davis, of course. So it's Maz?'

' Maz. I'm willingly stuck with it. And you've willingly come to room 208 at – ' she glanced at her watch – ' around midnight. I wonder why you came. I expect you do too. Mr Guy Bridges.'
She spoke clearly. An elegant cultured voice, Anglo–Indian RP, as if reading something from memory:
" With his first book, Past It, Bridges burst on to the so –called self development scene with a stellar presence. A scene so overcrowded it was turning in to a global in-joke was rejuvenated by one book, one presence. Precious it most certainly was not. Unprecedented it most certainly is. His second book, A Different Change confirms Mr Bridges is no one hit wonder. Even if Bridges, for whatever reason never wrote another book…"

' Funky? You're connected?'

' I'm not with you ?'

' Sorry. A personal reference. Do continue with whatever source you are drawing on.'

"… Even if Bridges, for whatever reason never wrote another book, his place at the top of this publishing category called self-development would be assured. Indeed his very stature and class call into question the triteness of this designation self – development. With Bridges lineage seemingly stretching back to philosophes such as

Rousseau, Voltaire, Emerson as well as parallel to present day stars, the Deepaks, the Robbins de nos jours. It is not the place here to find the well from which such wisdom is drawn, rather to discuss" -here Maz seemed to stop her imaginary reading and held Guy's gaze- " the future. The organising, the globalisation, indeed if I may be so vulgar, the branding of A Different Change begins now."

' Where did all that come from ?'

' The Observer, last month.'

' What is this? Who are you? What do you want?'

' The question, obviously, Mr Bridges, is what do you want? Why are you here? Would you prefer I was back in my white bra or blue one or none ? What is your agenda? What are you developing?'

Guy stood up to leave.

' It wouldn't be wise to leave now, Guy…'

' A threat?'

Maz laughed. It was really quite attractive. Guy could leave but he didn't. A neologism came into his head: mazmerised. He wanted to write it down – force of habit as a writer with new ideas – but he didn't want to have to explain himself to Maz. What he really wanted – Mr Number One best seller – was to be told what to do. That was why he had knocked on this door in this hotel in this, his hometown. He had come to be told what to do.

4

' What da Funk!' Funky always loved this chorus, the office catch–phrase as he strode in at the crack of 2pm.

' You're early,' smiled his PA, Ax. So called because no one in Funky's office had an attention span long enough to say Alexandra and for her tendency to axe into the end of other people's sentences.

' I'm on time. You're early. Whatsup?' responded Funky.

' Interview. Tatler, now. This evening, Late Review, live, live-ish.'

' Panel?' asked Funky.

' You, Beauty Mirror woman and Guy Bridges.'

' Bridges. I didn't kn…'

' Late review, late revision. Another panellist pushed off after Sunday Times bestseller results revealed. It's a biggy, Funk. Don't Funk up. Now, Tatler.

Let's pitch.'

' Did I know about this interv…?'

' Carried over from last week. You were too jet lagged or something after the Seattle gig. Yeah, and remember today I'm leaving early. Previous engagement.'

' Early?'
' I told you Funk. You may be the most fascinating man but you are a total bastard to work for.'

' But…who is he?'

' Her name is Maz since you asked. We often meet Tuesdays. Evidently the weekend isn't long enough for her.'

' But…me…'

' Yeah I love you too Funk, but life's too short. Press pressing. Tatler time. Let's pitch.'

5

Guy couldn't remember the last time he had stayed up so late. Outside the hotel window the birds began twittering; reminded him of Christ Church meadow for some reason. He used to be quite a night owl. Now it was early to bed, early to rise. The schedule demanded it, his pushing 50 body demanded it and most importantly he believed in it. Deep and regular sleep patterns were always featured in Guy's books and he walked his talk. If it had been 4 pm instead of 4am he probably wouldn't have even listened to Maz at all let alone agree to her schemes for world domination that would have made even a Blofeld look parochial.

' I can understand it's late and this meeting has been unconventional,' said Maz, ' but I'm going to sum up what we've agreed. This field is dominated by you and Funky – literature, TV, seminars, web casts, whatever. You want to remain number one. You are going to set up a franchise with me using the Guy Bridges imprimatur outside Europe. I can use my contacts with Funk's PA to feed you inside info on his moves and deals. If you want. If you're smart. You'll always be a step ahead. When the franchise is really established I resign. Solo time. My goal is to become dispensable to you – at the right time. You know it makes sense.'

' But I've always played with a straight bat…'

' We've agreed. You know it makes sense. You really are a nice guy, I mean that,' said Maz, moving closer to him, ' but you don't want to come second now do you?'

6

Guy was late on the Late Review set. Not hugely late in terms of time management, late enough to feel slightly flustered, to give the initiative to other people.

' Not like you,' was the only comment from Toby, BBC producer.

' Kings Cross,' was Guy's only response. After three deep breaths he was Guy Bridges again, best seller, guru, life –changer.

' Line up,' said the producer ' is you, Beauty Mirror woman, Funky. You cool with that?'

' Yeah,' lied Guy. The Beauty Mirror woman was unsettlingly beautiful. Funky was Funky.

The author of the best selling and critically acclaimed neo-feminist treatise Beauty Mirror was Natasha Lake. Beautiful, intellectual, incisive, able to move gracefully between radio, television and senior common rooms. Except for caligynephobic dons. She had become immensely successful very quickly but was almost always followed around by questions of varying explicitness probing at a connection between her own objective beauty and the subject of beauty she wrote about in her book. She arrived with an unfussy elegance and took her designated place in the line up next to Funky. The studio lights were getting hotter.

' Incidentally,' said Toby there is something I want to pitch to you. Something about doing what you do on air, real time, for real.'

' Later,' said Guy, ' we'll talk later. God these lights.'

Suddenly Funky and Guy were face to face. To describe the handshake as perfunctory would be overdoing it. Guy actually liked Funky. Funky didn't seem to like Guy. Not his type. He had some respect for him, but he didn't know the extent of it The problem was mutuality. Funky was never any good at stage sharing. It didn't matter if all the world was a stage. Funky's objective was to get Guy off it. Guy wasn't totally aware of the effect he had on Funky. Surprising really, given Guy's field was awareness.

' Been a while,' drawled Funky neither friendly or hostile.

' Yes, we did an Omnibus special a few years back. Went rather well if I remember.'

' For you,' muttered Funky. One of the additional unpleasant factors about Funky was his memory. He was capable of short-term lapses, especially when it suited him. But long term he collected an album of grievances, major, minor, perceived.
 The Omnibus special had left Funky feeling second best. It was in the same studio as the one they were going to use today, Studio 7. The Omnibus programme was more suited to Guy's style. He was smoother, more polished, the accent, the tie, the idioms. The programme gave a profile of their work so far. Then there was a segment for each of them to illustrate a facet of their work with the audience. Guy went first, asked for a volunteer from the audience and asked them if there was anything in their life they wanted to change. All he did was listen. In television terms the silences were vast. Finally Guy summed up, putting not the content but the tone back to his guest. It was spot on.

By contrast Funky looked like a fairground huckster. He didn't ask for a volunteer but chose a woman from the audience, didn't ask her what she wanted or anything so crass, but began to barrack her. What messages did she think she was giving out, her vocabulary, her over-acrylic dress sense, her tag question speech pattern. Then told her what she should do to move on, to be a new you. The woman broke down into tears. The camera cut away. It didn't look dramatic or cathartic, just nasty. Funky knew it. He had put it into his album of memories, of slights, of times when, ultimate crime, he perceived he'd come second.

7

At first sight you might not think of Guy Bridges as the UK's, if not the world's number one self help guru. But then what is a self help guru supposed to look like? Guy was tall, well spoken, that dash of the fighter pilot about him. You almost expected to hear him say " chocks away" or " pranged the kite" rather than " if you don't live your life to the full today tomorrow you will only have regrets " or " be yourself, who else could you possibly be?" His clothes gave him a more European than military look. Those complicated wiry specs you see middle level HR managers wear, longish but smart, centre parted hair, the young old face of an original Rolling Stone. The contradictions were fascinating, possibly revealing – the high collar Nehru jacket with the Oxford lace-ups. Now as for the designer label bedecked Funky….
' Lights, signature tune, five , four…' said the director. It was live TV.

8

Alex sat really close to Maz on the sofa. The Krug was in an ice box next to them, although the bottle was in use so much it was rarely actually in the box.
' There is such a chemistry between Bridges and Funk,' remarked Maz.

' Yeah, and it's all negative. Feels like the TV is going to fuse.'

' Negative chemistry is better than no chemistry. It can always be used, turned round. And it makes good TV. This prog would be on More4 at midnight if it wasn't for these boys.'

' God, what is Funk wearing?' Alex had already moved on. ' That bloody beret, those bloody trainers, it's enough to drive you to drink.'

' Like Nixon and Kennedy.' Maz continued on her track.

' What are you on about, you posh bitch?' said Alex amicably.

' Guy is so fresh looking, the crisp shirt, the lace ups. And your man in his shadowy, shady beret and …'

' My man?'

' Well he isn't mine, darling.'

' And the chemistry between us?'

9

The programme opened smoothly, just as you'd expect. Round table introductions followed by format presentation. Beauty Mirror woman first, then Funky, Guy bringing up the rear. Two way interviews with presenter on their work. Who had influenced them, an achievement they were most proud of, a technique from their own book they could most profitably apply to themselves. A round table wrap. Very tight, 30 mins max. The trouble began after Funky's segment. Funky knew the guidelines and the gentlemen's agreement to keep to time. The problem was Funky wasn't a gentleman. It worked two ways. Funky gave live TV, especially prime time, a just on the rails frisson but he was professional enough, when it suited him, to know where the line was.
' Thanks Funk,' steered the Late Review presenter.' Now, Guy Bridges. Practitioner, presenter, facilitator, author. Riding high in the best seller lists…'

' You know the Beauty Mirror deserves to be debated full on,' cut in Funky. 'Bridges is a derivative prat. Let's talk about women.'

' Cool it Funk,' said the presenter. ' You know the score. Guy Bridges. A Different Change, the new best seller. Influences?'

' No, let Funky continue his track.'

' Nice operating Guy,' opined Maz from the sofa. ' Funky is going to…'

' Walk right into it. Oh God. Isn't their anything under his beret?' Ax thrust the empty Krug bottle neck first into the icebox.

Funky didn't disappoint. If it was part of a Get Bridges strategy it wasn't clear.
Funky swivelled round in the studio chair so his back was to Guy. He addressed his fellow panellist.
' How do you think your book The Beauty Mirror would be different if you weren't so beautiful?'

' God, what kind of question is that? Ever heard of the word original, Funk?' was Natasha's response.

' A most revealing counter evasion,' said Funky in his most charming sneer.

' Thank you, Funky, thank you. Let's keep to our brief. Now Guy…'

' What is the point,' resumed Funky, ' what is the point of live TV if we can't-'   at this point he stared pointedly at the Beauty Mirror woman –' pursue conversations to limits, outcomes. So Bridges got the number one slot. It just about sums him up. He's a salesman. Am I the only one who can see through him?'

10

Maz seemed so unfazed by the drama unfolding on the screen in front of them that Ax began to develop Krug induced paranoia.
' Has someone spiked Funk's green room drink? Have you and Guy put this on?'

' Funk puts himself on, darling. Let Funk be Funk.' smiled Maz. ' I wonder where this will go.'

Back in TV land, the presenter had lost control. Funky had his back to them all except Beauty Mirror woman. He was ranting, saying over and over again: " beauty is all that matters, beauty is all that matters." The programme came to a lively end, with a close up of a calm, smiling, unaffected Guy, powerfully silent.

' Thank you all,' closed the presenter, secretly pleased at the notoriety taking place on his live slot. 'A most revealing half hour. We can look forward to the Guy Bridges hour special – uninterrupted – an exclusive broadcast soon.'

' Oh God, Oh God, Oh God, Oh Funk.' moaned Ax, now lying full length on the sofa as Maz glided about the room smiling with the sort of calm that irritates rather than reassures. ' If Funk goes down, I go down too. I never learn. Always hitch myself to his type, thinking it's more fun, then learning the hard way. It's too tiresome.'

' No one is going down. On the contrary,' said Maz. 'We are all going up.'

' You've lost it. You've had too much to drink. I haven't had enough.'

' I've had exactly the right amount to drink, my dear Alexandra. It is of course obvious. We are all going up. You, me, Guy…and Funky.'

' How so, Mazzo?'

Maz, sipped her Krug. ' You see, it's like this…'

 In TV studio – lucky for some – 7, the atmosphere was subdued.
' Cheers Funk. Always a pleasure to work with a real professional,' Toby almost screamed across the floor at Funky's departing back.

' You got what you wanted. Life is live. Bridges is a bad scene.'

' He never said or did anything.'

' Exactly, I do it all. Drama, content, ratings. Leave it to Uncle Funk. If you need me we'll be in the Met.'
He swung through the double doors, arm in arm with Beauty Mirror woman.

' Maybe nice guys do finish third,' was Guy's only comment. Maybe it's true thought the producer; calm people can really hang you up.
The silence continued. Guy made no attempt to break it. Silence is good. Finally Toby said:

' now Guy, old fruit, that something I want to pitch to you.'

II

1

The digital clock glowed. 2 AM. Maz was still on full alert. Post Krug, post Ax, Post studio 7. She was in bed, all alone with chapter two of A Different Change. It was the second time she had read the book but it seemed more alive now, more relevant. She had the feeling that something was about to happen. She wanted to be prepared.

Maz's Belsize Park pad was cool, but because that was how people expected her living space to be visitors never commented on it. Maz was not a woman given to disappointments nevertheless she felt the absence of compliments. Subtle lighting, a zebra rug on the plain blue woollen carpet, interesting juxtaposition of artwork. Posters by Hockney, Vuillard, Rothko with some original abstract watercolours by herself. They were good. Compliments about herself, her poise, her appearance, her sexual presence flowed. Not beautiful. Magentic. With effort, if she wanted to be.

She caught herself in the mirror.

'At least I have the decency to have a decent arse,' she said to herself, a propros, apparently, of nothing in particular.

Comments about and by herself. About the environment she had created around her, nothing.

Maz was drawn to Chapter 2. The Act of Balancing:

' If you get out of your own way you will always know when you are doing the right thing. Don't plot, gravitate. Be yourself, be your skills, mix with people who are going where you want to go. Orbit with stars.'

Yes, orbit with stars. A few years of moving in those circles would do nicely.

2

Maz was right. Something big was about to happen. She and Guy were going on a world tour. Together – at least initially. Guy had agreed to the franchise idea. Maz called it project 208. Here's how it was going to work. Maz came from a background of corporate HR. In her favour was her experience of presenting, training, motivating and holding large audiences. She had presence. She needed content. Over the next month she would work closely with Guy adapting material from his books and developing techniques for running large-scale seminars. The seminars would need to be effective in a range of environments: public or private sector business, Quangos, NGOs, individuals. They would need to work in a vast array of inter –cultural environments, there was no scope for boo – boos. Prices would be high. Guy's accountant suggested for the corporate sector 750 euros per head per day with a socially responsible sliding scale when running the seminar for individuals. The price was high too for Guy and Maz. For him, every time he was out there, in a company, on a stage it was his name, his reputation, his being. For Maz it was the chance of her lifetime. To shine, to be herself, to make a global reputation in her own right, to make money. Eventually she would move out of Guy's orbit, his shadow, into her own universe. For now things were as they should be.

3

The preparation was going well. Guy was easy to work with. The material was, thanks to Guy's skill, well suited to delivery in large arenas. They were developing a flowing rhythm together: a healthy balance of night-owlism and early birding, although despite their proximity to the Heath they could probably have done with more fresh air.
There was definite chemistry between them. Not just sexual, although that crackled in the air. Looking at them from the outside you could pick up a sort of John Steed / Tara King vibe. There was always this frisson. Guy thought back to that time in room 208. The bra. He never saw Maz naked or anything like it. She was one of those people who was always immaculate but you never saw them do anything to make themselves so. Early morning or late at night, on warm evenings as she worked there was again that glimpse of strap, white or blue. Guy was fascinated. Mazmerised.
Once he reached out, but the phone went.

4

' Maz, it's Ax. You were right.'

' I'm sorry?' said Guy.

'Oh God. I'm sorry. I need to speak to Maz please?'

' Need?'

' Would it be possible to simply put Maz on without you making me feel inferior with your inflection?'

Guy put the receiver down and sauntered back to his study, gesturing silently to Maz that the call was for her. Maz picked up.

' Maz? Ax. Hey, you were right, we're both going up with our star men. I suggest you read the Tatler. Gotta run.'

' Alexandra, where are you?'
The background was animated. Sounded like a spoof tape you could play if you wanted someone to believe you were ringing from an absurdly cool party. Ice cubes clinking, flirty laughter, Quincy Jones soundtrack.

' Does it matter? Have fun. You only come this way once. Are you feeling me girl? We'll catch up with you somewhere on the planet.'

' Meaning?'

' You're supposed to be the quick one, Maz. World tour no less. Watch out on the US dates!' Maz was left listening to the dialling tone and wondering.
Maz was an avid reader of Tatler. It was her fantasy mag. Some men read newspapers by working back from the sports results. Maz read Tatler by working back from those photographs of people blinging at some ball or launch or whatever. Sometimes in the

past she was even in them. Her subscription copy had remained unopened for over a week, beneath her reading material in preparation for the tour. She threw off the pile of promotional material she'd studied from Deepak and Robbins and unearthed her magazine. On the cover, centre stage again Funky. It wasn't exactly what Maz wanted on the eve of their -Maz and Guy's - world tour. Funky did look good. Leaving one of London's smartest members only clubs in what are always captioned the small hours Funky seemed to be making it big. Of course he did still have on that damned beret, but he was accompanied by a strikingly beautiful woman.
Maz skimmed the first paragraph:

'There's no such thing as bad publicity and London's number two self development writer and promoter aka Funky seems set to retake the number one spot he believes to be his own. And to quote the master himself " if you believe it, it is". Funky's recent storm out of studio 7 after describing number one bestseller Guy Bridges as a prat seems to have done him no harm at all. On the other hand Guy " world tour" Bridges is still the world's most sensitive and successful guru in this field. Funky doesn't do sensitive. He does do…what he wants. And he believes doing what you want is the key to well being.'

Maz skipped to the end and stared at the dates of Funky's US tour. Then stepped out onto the balcony, her mobile auto-dialling Alex back.

5

Guy was in a buoyant mood. The TV show with Funky had left him unfazed. He was pleased with the way he had handled himself. Pleased he hoped without being smug. The most important thing was he acted in accordance with his principles. To let go, to be on the path, to trust the way events unfold, to facilitate the growth of others. Do the right thing without concern if others seemed to have more glory or simply did what they wanted without restraint or consideration. It was difficult to say if Guy's background was conventional or unconventional. What is the ideal CV for a guru?

From Leeds Guy had scraped in to Oxford. He did well by working hard, putting in office hours at the Bodleian. He seemed to be a summer person, a time of year when he neglected the library to watch cricket at the Parks and observe girls in the Botanical Gardens. There had always been something healthy about the way Guy watched. It wasn't creepy or voyeuristic, it was almost like a compliment to be in his sights. Most people are good at one sense or communication channel. At that time Guy wasn't a noticeably good speaker or conversationalist. He was a listener, an observer, a learner, an accumulator. He could be defined by what he was and by what he was not. Not flashy, pushy, hurried, calculating. He didn't see advantages for himself when other people were down. He would get there in the end. Reputations are not quickly made by being a good listener but he didn't have to worry about being witty all the time, about always being " on". What you see is what you get. In many ways an attractive package: his emotional intelligence coupled with being tall and handsome enough for there to be no question of mediocrity.

6

It was only days now before the start of their tour. Today's subject: neuro-linguistic programming. Maz was a willing learner. Guy was, as you would expect in his position, an accomplished teacher. At the moment most of the learning seemed one way. Maz was fascinated by Guy's exposition of NLP. He explained we all communicate and interact through a range of styles but it can be possible to discern in a person if they have a lead communication style: visual, auditory, kinaesthetic or even olfactory or gustatory. VAKOG. Maz thought of some of the people she new. Alexandra for example with her current catch – phrase " are you feeling me?" She began to notice signs and expressions around her. The features editor who said Funky's last book " stank". She thought about Guy, the listener. How sexy real listening is.

The thought had stayed in her mind. How sexy real listening is, building connection, a feeling of closeness.
'Guy?' said Maz at the end of their NLP session. She was feeling aligned, congruent, Lucky.

'Yeah,' drawled Guy. He'd moved on to checking the itinerary for the tour but as soon as Maz spoke he put down the files and looked straight back at her. Full on listening.

'Do you think I'm lucky to be going on this tour with you, or we are lucky to be going on this tour together.'

'Luck? Reminds me of what my mother once said way back. " Luck is like bread. You make it yourself."' Maz didn't recall hearing Guy talk about family past before. She went deeper.

'What's your take on coincidence, chance, things being meant to happen?'

'Why are you asking me that, or rather why are you asking me that now?'

' Oh, you know, the hotel room, us going on this tour, is this what is meant to happen?'

'You were at my book signing. You asked me to the room. I wasn't just passing. The tour, it's a business deal, we've both something to offer, to give, to gain, to learn.'

'That's it?'

' You mean about coincidence? Yes. I haven't worked out the mathematics of meetings by chance or design. That might be the sort of thing Fermat or Heisenberg would do, it isn't what I do. If you go solely in a mathematical direction you minimise the intent, responsibility side of things. Which is what I do. We will do. Meetings happen, occur. If you want to have some kind of theorem of coincidence where could you start from?'

'Meaning?'

' Take the hotel room in Leeds, us going on this tour together, anything. What time point could you possibly start from? Think about the tour as an example. Take a gig at random.'

'Rotterdam'

'Rotterdam, right. Who will be there? How did they find out about it? Supposing a flyer fell off a noticeboard and blew down the street. Someone who has never heard of Guy Bridges…'

'…Imagine that' said Maz.

Guy continued. The theme seemed to intrigue him. ' The flyer is blowing down the street. Someone happens to be in Rotterdam. May be their parents were, shall we say, lucky enough to escape a Nazi raid on their home and fetched up there or someone just got too boozed up to catch the ferry back to Hull. They are in Rotterdam, happen to be on the same street, the same side of the street as the paper, pick it up, can read the same language as the paper is written in, want to come to the gig and are free that very evening. That would be a coincidence, the starting point for the person picking up the paper because the wind blew it their direction.
But you'd have to start with the person being born, their parents, the parent's parents, all time leading up to that moment. No I don't believe in coincidence in that sense, that way madness lies.'

'So how do you explain things then?'

'Intersections. The intersection of time leading up to the event when you make the choice and therefore start your own journey. What interests me is the choices people make at and after our gigs, events, seminars, lectures, broadcasts, whatever. Before that there is only time. There comes a time when you can make a choice. Time is a perpetual nowness of choices.'

'Intersections. Interesting. Just imagine the hundreds of people reading the flyers, looking at the web site, planning to go to our events right now. All those hundreds of people out there, people who will intersect with us, people we might change, people who might change us.'

Guy was about to return to the planning. 'Not hundreds, Maz' he said, 'thousands, one day maybe even more. If all goes to plan that is,' Guy added with a winning smile.

7

' What da Funk!' It was that time of day again. Funky swept into his office. His working days were getting shorter as his working nights were getting longer.

' Whatsup?' he said to Ax, somewhat shortly.

' Hey, big man, it's me Ax, remember, R.E.S.P.E.C.T. Do you wanna know what Bridges is doing?'

' Who?'

' Nice try Funk, but he's still number one which makes you number tw…'

' And your point is?'

' You and Bridges are dividing up the world. Should be big enough for you both, doncha think? And that Maz woman. You know the one with the big …'

' That's so yesterday.'

' You mean you know about the dates or the cup size?'

' What dates?'

' Good answer, Mr New man. You and Bridges are going to be in the States at the same time. I've got their dates and venues.'

' I could kill Bridges. In fact….'

' Now, now, think of your reputation. Well. Maybe not. I'll fix it.'

'You're right the States is big enough for us both. Just fix it so we don't appear in the same place at the same time.'

Funky's ring tone trilled out.

' Yeah,' he snapped. It was a real mood, a black clouder affecting voice tone and brow and Ax noted, breath. She stepped back. Funky's mood altered as soon as he heard the voice on the line. 'Lake, babe,' he smiled. ' I'll be right there.'

Guy Bridges was higher self. Funky was lower self, everyone's shadow side. This was how Funky had become so successful in a field not obviously natural to him. A few years back he was between jobs, resting. He had made his post-Saint Martins money in what is now well known as world music. With his ability to create and ride trends he promoted world music before people knew it was a genre. He had contacts in the superclubs, the fashion houses, the style mags. He spotted the high potential of some of the bands coming out of Mali, Senegal. He discarded the losers and put together off-beat winners with established middle level rock names. It changed Funky from a successful odd job man into a mover. He made money quickly. Ax joined him first, from a PR house. Then he set up his office in Richmond. He was an interesting boss, coming and going apparently as he pleased although all his staff were on fixed hours. They even clocked in, no flexi, but as so often with Funky it was these contradictions that worked.

At the top of this venture Funky had become ill. There was no diagnosis. Ax thought he should just check into The Priory like everyone else, but Funky knew it was more than

that. Some of his more esoteric contacts gave him books. In the same way as there is now a genre called world music, there is now a genre called self development.
One of the things that surprised people around Funky was that he wasn't cynical. Everyone seemed to expect he would be but he wasn't. He read of how people had cured themselves of cancer or depression by positive thinking, left crap jobs and found what they really wanted to do when they faced down parents, siblings, ghosts and other tyrants. He chanted prayers, not to Jesus or Buddha, but to The Eternal Self or Source. It worked. Funky was back in business, it was a new age for him.

8

Guy, as was his general practice, had encouraged Maz to keep a journal. Write what she wanted, stream of consciousness, dreams or fantasies from waking or asleep, observations, hopes. One technique was to write grids of opposites.
Maz was a natural student, a natural student of this subject, a natural student of Guy's. In their Rotterdam hotel the night before their first big gig together she wrote:

' Guy: higher self, listener, George Harrison. In a film, played by Cary or Hugh Grant with sound track by Georgie Fame.
Colour: blue. Brand: YSL, Armani, Austin Reed.
Funk: lower self, shadow side. Keith Richards. In a film played by Dennis Hopper with soundtrack by Steely Dan. Colour: black. Brand: Not enough space.'

She began to write down something about fantasies. She noted Guy wasn't coming up. Then she crossed it out. Never write anything down you wouldn't want anyone else to see. The night passed with the aid of arnicas. Tomorrow was a biggy, not just the numbers but what it meant.

Guy and Maz had successfully run seminars in South and East London, Manchester and Edinburgh. Maz was doing more and more of the fronting although they were still recognisably a Guy Bridges event. The procedure rarely varied. Round circle introductions by Guy, ask a volunteer to relate a story, an experience, an issue that was coming up for them, a wish for change. Group work based on NLP, mentoring, transformational analysis. Listen to people speak, give them space, let them turn themselves round. Maz was learning to zap negativity. She began to genuinely enjoy the part of the seminars when people tipped from " I can't" or " people like me don't know that" or " it' s impossible because…" to " I can, I can't wait. I'm going to start now." Working closely together her respect for Guy grew. It wasn't just the way he worked, the almost mysterious way there seemed to be all the time in the world but the results attained in the time the seminar was allotted, the ratio of listening, speaking, guiding, his disinterest in power.
It was also the genuine achievements. You could see in people a before and after. Guy was generous in giving her space. She remembered that evening in Manchester when she moved someone forward, people smiling seconds after crying. Maz didn't share the disinterest in power.

Rotterdam was an ideal venue to take off the swimming wings, the tricycle stabilisers. Guy had worked here before. The highly educated, motivated, almost bilingual people but away from the hot house of London and the press which Guy attracted. Here everyone wanted success: Guy, Maz, the participants, the promoters, any attendant media. In London most people also wanted success, but some didn't. In the same way some people like to scratch Porsches, some were out to puncture Guy's calm.

9

Maz began well.
' I'm going to tell you three things about myself. Two true, one not. I was born in London, I once modelled for Yves St Laurent, grapefruit gives me a rash.'
It never failed. There was some amusement about the attempts to discuss the three statements in a politically correct way. Maz was still discernibly sub-continental, the complexion, the eyes, the Benazir Bhutto intonation. To say this was the lie would be to call her an immigrant. Although she had arresting poise she seemed too full breasted to be a fashion model. To say this would show that was what you had focussed on. The grapefruit point just seemed too banal – this was Guy Bridges' new star.
The discussion continued. Facilitation was all very well but Maz decided to show leadership.

' Time is running. What do you think?' she asked a striking woman in the second row. Come to think of it hadn't she seen her somewhere before?

' Grapefruit,' said the woman, tersely. Maz was miffed. Being right first time is always deflationary.

' And your reasoning?'

' People own where they are from too much to mess about. I saw your picture in Tatler in the YSL strapless thingy. It revealed so much of you.'

Maz noted the woman's command of barbed double meaning. The woman continued.

' The truth is often banal. Grapefruit.'

Maz managed a ' well done', realising the next step was of course to ask the participant who guessed correctly for their three items. Maz could feel the woman becoming an alternative power node. She glanced across at Guy who was in the room but only as a fly on the wall. Another power node too, she thought. I can handle it, I will handle it, I will enjoy handling it.

' Please go ahead,' she said, her intonation indicating the woman should give her name.

' Francoise.'

' Francoise. Please, your three. It will be fun.'

Francoise stood up. She had a boxy Chanel suit on, very news anchor. Within that merest hint of cleavage a subtly expensive silver necklace with a cross sparkled. What was more significant , wondered Maz, the low key display of assets or the cross? Lapsed Catholic? Convent school? God knows.
Francoise even seemed to welcome attention. The thought occurred to Maz why was she there? Often at these events there were people who wanted attention – hoggers –

Guy occasionally called them – but you could see through them. They were usually the first to start the tears.
It wasn't possible to see through Francoise.
She spoke so well. An accent-less international English.

' I was born in Lille. I play the cello. I'm addicted to TV.'
The whole room was locked onto her – Bridges most emphatically included.
The discussive hub- hub started up again. What could it be? She spoke English beautifully but it was too arid to be a native speaker. Lille was just off beat enough to be plausible. Cello, yes, the instrument for sensitive intellectuals, you could just imagine the 2 AM arpeggios cascading down a Left Bank stairwell. TV addiction? Crass, sort of thing that could creep up on you if you were too much of a health fanatic to get wrecked up with something you take internally. Maz broke with tradition and didn't put the exercise out to the audience. She felt Guy looking at her.

' TV addict.'

' That obvious, is it?' remarked Francoise. When she smiled she looked like someone else. Warmer, someone you could hug. The nonsmiling version just looked like a smart arse. Maybe she could become a TV addict, the discipline manifestly inherent in her a kind of dam that could easily crack. Maz smiled back.
Her surmise had reclaimed some power. She moved gracefully on to the next stages, and soon had people buzzing away in pairs or breakaway groups. Maz and Guy monitored, supported cathartics, summarised outcomes. Rotterdam was a success. They moved on, a city every night, names you see on a rock tour tee shirt: Hamburg, Berlin, Stockholm, Bergen, a trans Europe express of welcomed tears.
She wrote in her journal:

' What predominant feeling am I saying hello to? Pride.'

10

In the Richmond office Ax had not clocked off. She had assumed a lead PR function, working late with the team on promoting Funky's tour. It was exhilarating and exhausting but she was looking forward to it. She was remembering what she was good at, journalism, style, design, making it happen, being out there. Funky knew Ax was the best and let her get on with it. But he had given her their angle for the tour: Hard Caring. Tears were for crybabies. Tears weren't cathartic they were just soft. Get a grip. Decide, what you need to do, who you need to be, who you need to know.
Posters were designed. Press releases primed, polished by the superb prose of Nash Lake. Ax worked on the all important slogan, the brand.
Even later, when even the most un needy of sleep had retired to the inner suburbs, Ax picked up the phone.
' Maz, you there? Pick up. Get this, you know what we're gonna call the tour?
" Hard Funk: In Your State." Pick up Maz. Or may be it's too late, you're out there in self help land with no one to help you. No Alexandra. I hope it's what you want Maz. I hope you hitched yourself to the right guru.'

Ax had worked for or with Funky since those world music days. When they set up a company and moved into the office in Richmond she almost moved on. Although

Funky could be infuriating he was creative, sparky, no three days were ever alike. They were an effective partnership. Funky the product, Ax a creative director, keeping Funky on the right side of implosion, having fun, making money. She enjoyed moving in their eclectic world, the swirl of musicians, writers, painters, fashion, PR. An office and Funky sometimes seemed a contradiction, but she learned the only way to really enjoy chaos and stay healthy over a longer term was to be organised. Ax had an innate confidence, more street than quad, and was at home in her world. She met Maz at a launch. Couldn't remember now what was being launched. She had gone with a man, couldn't remember who. But she wanted to leave with Maz. It was a different change.

You travel the world; conference centres, TV studios, radio shows, flash hotels. Things happen. Even if they don't you think they should. Ought. If you don't want to feel disappointed, it's all over for you. you're not a player. Strange as it may seem, Guy and Maz were rarely alone together now. There was always a third party – a promoter, an exec, someone who came up to you post-gig and didn't understand the etiquette about leaving. They were back at the hotel. Somewhere in Europe, Brussels, Rotterdam, Uppsala. Maz couldn't remember the place. You know the cliché about hotels being samey. It gets to be true.

As long as you are walking along the corridor together everything is fine. The decision is ahead of you but you don't have to take it for at least 10 steps, 8, 5, 3…
Maz had her hand on the door handle of her hotel room. Looking back Guy remembered he couldn't remember the room number. Her hand began to press the door handle down. She didn't exactly say ' what's it to be Guy, you make the call, a decision, do something you can't get back from.' Not out loud. The door was ajar now. Her open wardrobe was reflected in the entrance hall mirror. The door was wide open. She held his gaze, her eyes gleaming. Guy didn't look away. He held her in his arms then kissed her firmly, decisively, on the cheek.

III

1

' What da Funk!' was the chorus greeting him everywhere he went. Funky loved it. Ax had told him Bridges was travelling in the US by train. The environmentally friendly softy. Funk was blasting from city to city, state to state by private jet.
' Doncha just love it?' said Funky to Ax as they disembarked. 'Where are we? Why are we where we are? Tell me but don't stop smiling.' Funk, Ax and Nash descended the steps, photographers in their face.

' Philadelphia. One lecture, one book signing.'

' What's the lecture about?' asked Funky.

' You tell me. Same one as you gave last night I suppose.' Ax continued smiling as paparazzi flashed in her face. People wanted to know who she was too. A muse, a lover, a disciple? It had all happened so quickly. Ax had arranged a prime time talk show host to attend the first of Funky's " Hard States" happenings. Then at the flagship

event at the New York Plaza Funky had accidentally on purpose chosen the editor of Vogue to be his " victim." No one had ever, at least publicly called such an eminence a " hollow bitch" before. Next day she called up Funky. Ax handled the call. The editor had thanked Funky for " taking her apart." Ax listened then closed the call:
' it's a pleasure.'

After that the PR looked after itself. The TV talk shows that mattered, those radio stations with weird alphabetic names, web casts. Funky was even offered an extraordinary slot on a late night satellite show " In the Jacuzzi with…" in which the guest presenter, in this case Funky, interviewed guests in the whirl of the pool, presumably a subliminal image of the stream of the playful mind. Funky was adept at inviting features editors, women, not so much into bed but into the whirlpool. This happened to be after Lake had been recalled to Oxford for a seminar series at Templeton. Things were always happening. Funky was big, and with him Ax.

2

Funky looked out from his lectern. No one, not even Bridges would dare to hold pauses like he did. Ax looked on from the wings. It felt like they were on some kind of brink, the pauses were so infinite. At his lectures there were no coughs, sweet wrappers, rival nodes.

' I'm not going to thank you for coming,' was Funky's provocative opening.
' We are not here to play games. You will all leave here today as different people. You are all liars, frauds, you live behind a front. Is there any one here who will challenge my assumption?' Funky stood out from behind the lectern. Alex always thought there would be an evening when there would be a challenge, like that moment in a wedding when the vicar intones speak now or forever hold thy silence. Silence was always held. Funky's nerve always held.
' So we are all together. Complicit. What do you want me to do? Do you expect to hear a universal truth from me? There isn't one. That is the truth. Do you want to stay the same? Continue living your lies, veneers. That isn't an option any more. Time's up. Simply by coming here you have chosen to leave that behind. Take a deep breath and feel the relief. Time's up. I'm not going to give you an analysis. Analysis is a synonym for excuse. Everyone in this hall knows what I mean. Excuses. This is a city of excuses.' Here Funky simply inserted the name of the evening's city. ' Philadelphia is a city of excuses. Parents, school, sex, too much, not enough, wrong sort. Other people, children, politicians, celebs, illegals, medics, advertisers, other people. There are no other people. There is only one person, you. Therefore how can there be excuses? Here's what you're going to do. We are going to sit in silence for 5 minutes. We start now.'

As they crossed the states Ax waited for the challenge. The person who would interrupt. The audience that couldn't last those five minutes. It is almost impossible to imagine how long a silence of 5 minutes is in a huge auditorium. It never happened. Night after night. Funky's lecture. The only variation the insertion of the city name. The silence always held. It was so powerful. Funky simple stood still and stared back into the lights, the not so benign silhouette.
' Give yourselves a round of applause,' said Funky when he received the time up signal from the off stage Alex, imperceptible to the audience. It was so empowering.

' Your old life, your life of excuses is over. Take a deep breath, stand up, embrace your brother or sister next to you, embrace your new life, your big life, your lie-less life. Now walk. Go.'

With this Funky was gone, the silence in the hall more rapturous than the most thunderous applause.

3

Very late the next morning, Funky and Ax woke up. He was in bed with the deputy principal features writer of an upmarket fashion-meets-health-meets wealth mag. Which title was it? She had told him but he felt now it would be rude to ask again. She might think he didn't listen.
It was an uptown New York day. She was reading the New York Times.
' I'll give you one guess who is number one in the non –fiction bestseller list,' she teased. ' If you get it right you can…'

Across the continent in Santa Monica, Ax was in bed with their new West Coast agent Martine.
' I'll give you one guess who is number one in the LA Times non-fiction best seller list,' Martine said softly, caressing Ax. 'If you get it right first time you can….emmm, you do that real swell, you English girls.'
It was nice, it was true. Funky was number one coast to coast.

4

' Alexandra, pick up, pick up, it's Maz. Which side are you on. Sorry – I mean which side of the world are you on? God it's late, er no it's early. Are you…?'

' Nice of you to call, Maz, what's all this about picking up?' said Ax.

' You sound very on.'

'You sound very about to do something big and scary.'

' Percipient of you. You go first. What have you been doing? Who has been doing what to whom?'

' You're not being crude are you now, naughty Maz, but I like it.'

' Like what?'

' Oh. Double meanings too! My! Yes, right. You want me to go first. I'm in Santa Monica.' Ax actually held the receiver out of the sliding doors. She'd seen some starlet do that in a film. ' Can you hear the ocean?'

' No.'

' Wouldn't have been difficult for you to say yes. But, hey, no questions, no lies. So we're here in Santa Monica.'

' We?'

' I thought the theory was you do these things 10 minutes each way with no interruptions. But since you're so curious, Martine and me…'

' I.'

' What?'

' Martine and I, Ax, Martine and I. I thought you were trying to better yourself.'

' Martine and I are just playing, by the sea, the waves are crashing…'

' Right, Missy, if you are going to play games…'

' Flirting is in, haven't you read the literature?'

' Let's talk business. What are you doing in Santa Monica? And where the Funk is Funky?'

' I'm a sherpa. Funky is red-hot coast to coast. He's flying in here tomorrow. Biggy. Hollywood Bowl. You gotta believe it. Martine and I are getting , sorry, putting it together. Do you think I just lie around thinking about your breasts all day? Why are you giving me 'tude? You went off with the other man, remember, remember?'

' I said business. What is Funk doing? How has this all come about?'

' Opposites. Bridges is Bridges the listener, the healer, the straight bat. Let Funky be Funky. He lectures them. Tells them. Listening is so last year.
You still there?'

' Go on.'

' The secret is lectures. Tell 'em. They love it. No excuses. Embrace your brothers and sisters, stand up, live your lie-less life. I've said enough. Funky would kill me. Funky has this fierce rule, participants sworn to secrecy. They keep it. They do what he tells them. Your turn. Let me guess where you are. Dulwich, Leeds, Rotterdam even '

' Sydney.'

This time there was a silence.
' Way to go girl! Whatssup?'

' Guy and I started out, you are right, in South London. Bridges kept his word. He taught me so much. I went solo in Rotterdam. Plaudits all round. We split the world. Me, Australia Pacific, Bridges is North America.'

' Scared?'

' I was at first. Felt the fear and did it anyway. I love it.'

' So why are you so lonely?'

' What are you talking about?'

' I can hear it. You're by the Pacific too, but there is no smile in your voice. Hey, I know this great speaker, he'd…'

5

Guy was training all over the East Coast. It was a natural environment for him. Maz had tipped him off. Leave the West Coast flakes to Funky was the advice. In the observation car he looked up from his laptop and peered out across the brilliant trees of New England. He was pleased with the way things were going. A smile flickered across his face as he remembered room 208. Maybe that is what he needed at that stage. In his worldview people appeared for a reason. He had worked alone for all of his ascent to his current eminence. Maz was just unconventional enough to be a fitting partner. He needed to keep learning to stay on the journey rather than assuming he'd arrived. Guy was a guru, not a saint. Money, bestseller lists, TV ratings, style and approbation from peers in the profession were not without interest. The trees flashed past.

" I am on the path, I am on the path " was his silent chant in time to the chatter of the rails.

Guy was proud too of his dealings with Maz. The franchise idea was sound business. The frisson energised his work. He shared all his seminar and coaching techniques with her unreservedly, but she wasn't his creature. He noticed her making the material her own. After Rotterdam she flew off like a released butterfly. Where was she now? He glanced at the date on his Breitling. Melbourne, no that was a few days ago. Sydney. Yes, the Opera house, the sound of the waves, the open air restaurants with their crisp table cloths and fresh, health giving food. What was she doing now? Working - in front of the groups, her attractive vulnerability, the top three buttons on her white blouse undone. Or sleeping, reading, writing? Guy glanced at his rail timetable. 25 minutes to arrival. He hypnotised himself into a light sleep, the train gliding on through the colours. Guy remerged as the train entered Baltimore station.

6

At each station the routine was reassuringly repeated. Met by the promoter and driven to the venue. Posters outside the hall. Guy Bridges: A Different Change, with full-face photograph. Again Guy asked himself a wisdom access question. " Was he vain?" Before he had time to confront his own question he was greeted by his East coast agent: ' Mr Bridges. Louisa-May, we've spoken on the phone so many times, it's such an honour to see you. We are all looking forward to an inspirational evening.'

Guy held her eyes, restraining himself from moving his eyes up and down her figure. Louisa- May knew it and registered an uncalled for minor disappointment, perhaps like a woman in high heels walking past a building site unremarked.

' The pleasure is mine. It's such an honour to be in the States, to be travelling, sharing. This tour has been inspirational so far. It just keeps getting better.'

Guy and Maz had standardised their routine. If you were at a Guy Bridges seminar in New England or a Maz Khalm seminar in New South Wales the objective experience was the same- in theory. Logos, handouts, flow as branded as Apple or Virgin, every continent, every time.

Louisa-May began the proceedings.
' It is a pleasure to welcome among us this evening, from London, England Mr Guy Bridges. He is a man who needs no introduction, we feel we know him already through his work. It is truly wonderful to have with us in real time a presence known to us, however warmly, through the channels of articles, books, talk shows. We are looking forward to the evening, our journey, a different change. Ladies and Gentlemen, Mr Guy Bridges.'
Guy stepped forward, smiling, gesturing with a flat palm for the applause to stop.
The hall was full. 80% women 20% men. Two TV crews with lights, a digital video crew Guy and Maz had organised for the forthcoming DVD.
Guy had done this so many times now, but there was no room for complacency. This business was like journalism or the theatre: you're only as good as your last article or performance. It would be too easy for critics to fling back quotations from his books:

" if you tread water you will surely sink."

" if you are not delighted by your own work, why should anyone else be?"

Guy smiled, picking out friendly faces in the middle to back rows for extended eye contact.
' Thank you, Louisa – May. Your introduction is most kind. The warmth of the reception on this tour of your lovely state has been deeply moving. We are exchanging energy, I feel I am among friends, people I know, people who know me. But however many times you may have read my work, seen me on TV, heard about me from others there is always more to know, more layers to peel down. Here is a simple warm up for us. I'm going to tell you three things about me, two true, one untrue. Let's see what you can guess. Here goes. I was born in a city called Leeds, in the north of England, my favourite rock group is the Rolling Stones, I believe in miracles.'
Guy smiled as the buzz started. Partnerships formed, groups normed, here they were with Guy Bridges Live in the USA deciphering his truths. One of the men in the hall called out he'd been to Leeds.'
' Hell of a nice place, real close to hush hush place on the moors where I was stationed before I joined the Peace Corps.'
The usual Beatles v Stones dichotomy opened up between a group of woman recalling their sorority days at University in Boston. It seemed plausible a man of Guy's vintage would like The Stones, the rhythm, the sex, the model of active ageing, but maybe it was just a red herring. Miracles. Of course he would believe in miracles, he had changed so many people so profoundly. Guy closed the buzz again with that flat palm movement.
The consensus seemed to be The Stones were the bad boys of his trio of truths. He really seemed more like a Schumann or Schubert man. You could just see him, in a panelled study, sipping Montrachet, listening to The Trout. No one had even discussed

the miracle issue. Guy did the eye contact thing again. You had to hold eye contact even longer in the US than in Europe.

' I don't believe in miracles.' It seemed almost shocking. ' There are no miracles,' he intoned evenly three times. A silence was held but then broken. A man stood up. The cancer stories came, from men and women. Guy welcomed it.

' You did it yourselves, you did it through love, you did it through belief. Belief in yourselves, the belief others have for you. It is wondrous, it is joyous, it is not miraculous.'
The buzz flickered up again.
Some people wanted to believe in miracles, some people were not yet ready for contradiction, controversy, unsettling.
Guy picked these people out and repeated again in a low level tone:

' You did it yourselves, you did it through love, you did it with belief. There are reasons, there are methods, they can be learned.' The silence returned. Guy analysed the silence, it was accepting not hostile. He began to move forward, to work deeper, to take people with him, to do what he did. At Guy's instigation working groups were formed, mentors appointed, toolkits explained and unpacked, transformations begun. Guy invigilated around the room, supporting gently, intervening at pivotal moments. Cases emerged. The woman who had been a jazz singer for 20 years but really wanted to make it as a librarian. The man in his 50s told he would never work again but had a novel business idea. The well-dressed woman with the elaborate hairstyle who looked centred but said she was immobilised with feelings of unworthiness and hooked on meaningless one-night stands. As the evening progressed tears began to fall. Guy was well versed in seeing the signs. The calm discussions, the non-judgemental support listeners gave to speakers, people with arms round each other, genuine, non-threatening. Then you saw a body shudder, a silence, then tears. It always amazed Guy how many different ways there were to cry. Some people appeared almost to be laughing, others seemed to be in a sort of sexual ecstasy, others heaved their shoulders emitting a noise like a sea lion. Some were distressed because they couldn't cry, like being stuck on the edge of an orgasm. Guy knew innately what to do. The delicate interventions, the simple touch, a magic word. Tears gave way to smiles, hunched shoulders to straight backs, tension to ease. People began to hug each other, moving around with excitement or remaining still with new found peace. Often Guy relinquished the microphone for participants bursting to make announcements. Cognac, cigarettes, cocaine and other absurd crutches – " I can't think why I ever needed these things" – were cast aside. Businesses were started there and then, ambitions and dreams turned into plans even the most cynical bank manager would regard as watertight. Language changed from " I can't" or " it isn't me" to " I am, I will." Couples about to scrap years of half-life together were invigorated, new joint projects stretching out in front of them, equipped to start right NOW. Guy was there among it all, happy, alive, never complacent about what he had facilitated. His wrap up always short, always the same:

' I am happy you no longer need me. This change is different. This change is forever.'

The applause rose, led by Louisa-May. He clapped back the way Communist politburo chiefs clapped back at the masses. The lights rose, the cameras cut.

As Guy wended his way out of this hall of energy only one figure disturbed his equilibrium. A striking figure in profile powerfully dressed, glint of a necklace with a silver cross. Sitting, unclapping, two rows back, the woman in the Chanel suit, her tears still flowing, her silence definitely not golden. An intersection? Seizing the time, Guy turned towards her, his hand outstretched:

'Guy Bridges'
The woman faced him full on, shook hands on equal terms, her hand so slightly moist from – Guy tried to sense it – tears, scent, fear, power?
'Francoise du Pont'
'Have to hurry hustle' ushered Louisa – May indicating the door, the outside world.

7

Louisa – May dropped Guy at his hotel, Guy making her good-night kiss short and non-lip. Louisa – May didn't just leave it at that. There are kisses and there are kisses. 'If you want to talk I'm the best listener in America' said Louisa – May.

'I'm sorry?' said Guy.

'Does that mean " sorry" as in sorry or sorry as in "excuse me" can you repeat that please? You can be very obtuse sometimes you Brit guys.'

' I mean what does you are the best listener in America mean?'

' OK, maybe second best listener is more correct. I did learn the listening skill from your seminars. So what do you want to talk about? What do you want me to listen to?'

' I don't follow you,' said Guy.

' Evidently. Let me confront you with something. How did you learn to kiss like that? There's more warmth from a woodpecker's beak than from your lips.'

The leaves rustled. There was a chill in the night. It was that time when you could go home, see if sleep came and the next morning was the next morning, same as the one before. Or you could see where the night went.
The door slid back and Guy stepped into the people carrier Louisa - May had hired for the event. The black windows superfluous at this hour. Inside were various brochures, flyers and reviews of Guy's East Coast Tour:

" Inspirational"
" A Different Change – You may want to go back but you won't need to"
" Listen to Guy Bridges, Listen to Yourself."

Outside the carrier Louisa – May drew the door back. Unnoticed by both, the Bridges Tour poster fell from door to the ground as the car sped back to Louisa – May's hotel.

Of course it had to be room 208 of the local Howard Johnson. Guy ordered up a Becks, Louisa- May a Campari and soda. It was the first time Guy and Louisa – May had been alone in a room together. As his East Coast agent they had conversed for years, by phone, snatches of conversation in lobbies. Easy, flowing, trusting. She had always made everything so smooth for Guy in the USA. Things went so well she was never really noticed; could be an incentive to mess up, but then you'd only get noticed for the wrong reason and would only spend the attention time you gained explaining. Guy was beginning to wonder what it was about him and hotel rooms. Perhaps he could develop a different approach, throw the TV in the pool or…start a conversation with someone who went way back, but only by telephone.

Guy began, clear voiced despite the hour.
' You're right, your perception of the kiss is spot on, you deserve more'

' In depth kisses or deeper explanations?'

' I don't need to explain myself, Louisa – May,' said Guy ' I kiss who I want. So do you, so does anyone.' The tone came out avuncular almost prim rather than masterly. Guy didn't even like the tone of his own voice. A withholding voice. She was a good listener, a good person to talk to, why shouldn't it be her? She smiled and remained silent. Guy decided to assert himself over his passivity. It wasn't too late to start the journey. Guy continued, the tone right this time.
'Relationships. 15 minutes each way'

'Just what I wanted,' responded Louisa – May, red lips meeting the Campari,
' Late night stories. You start. I wonder where you are going to begin?'

It was 12 15 when Guy started.
'Do you know what GP means?'

'Not another of those crazy Limey – Yank things like suspenders and braces,' said Louisa - May smiling, enjoying the frisson of safe danger.

' General Practitioner. Medical Doctor, family doctor. My Dad was a GP in Leeds, big city in the north of England. Just after the war.'

'So it's your Dad,' said Louisa May.

' Sorry, I mean pardon?' said Guy.

' I wondered where you would begin. Father or mother. Looks like it's your Dad.'

Guy turned to pour out some more Becks but the bottle was empty. Louisa – May deftly passed him another one from the fridge.
' Thanks,' said Guy, ' we said 15 minutes each way and you were the best listener in America. You lasted 7 words before your first interruption.' The tone was coming right now. Guy continued.
' My Dad the GP was struck off. Struck off the list of those eligible to practise medicine. I was just about in my teens. You could smell, feel, taste the shame, for him, for his wife, my mother, me. Only child. He had had an affair, used his position as a GP to his advantage. That was the words of the inquiry. Always remember the words. Used his position to his advantage. He used his position.'

Guy talked fluently. Louisa – May could see it all. The family moving from town to town, trying to start again, to keep secrets from others while rebuilding their own bonds, if they could. Father to son, husband to wife, truths to themselves, to the world.
Who were they now? The respectable family, the professional status and income. Things were repaired, but never the same.
By 1230 Guy had revealed more to another person, revealed more to himself than he had for years and years.

'So that's it, Boss, that's why we just get the peck on the cheek.
You know that isn't good enough'

'I've tried to put you in the picture' said Guy

' I mean the 15 minutes. Start 1215. Finish 1230. Next, over to me. 12 45 you get a taxi to your hotel. It isn't good enough. Tell me the story again, without the limits. And don't think about the time. We can do my 15 uninterrupted minutes another night.'

The next evening Guy wrote in his journal:

'Premonition.'

Why did he feel that? He tried to analyse it, be rational rather than emotional. The tour was a success. In financial terms every night a sell out. His books, tapes and back catalogue snapped up. His agent offering him more
Gigs, bigger events, spectaculars. Critical acclaim. He looked through the reviews Louisa – May collected for him daily:

" Bridges is a modern day master."
"We can't call him a miracle worker, but the results sure are."
" 'I'd follow Guy around the world and beyond' – participant declares."

 If he wanted adulation he'd got it. The money was flowing in. True he was alone in yet another hotel but that was his choice. All around him acclaim, physical and financial manifestations of wealth, but the spiritual? He threw the reviews on his desk. They fell on the floor and opened at random:

" Battle of the Gurus – Funk ousts The Bridge as number one."
" Guru Brits in coast to coast play –off: Funky rocks L A."

 Guy left the reviews unheeded under the desk. It was getting late.

The hotel was completely silent. Outside there may be stars or trees but the window was just like a black plate. He searched the mini-bar but couldn't even decide what he wanted. It was the sort of hotel where you could have everything, but if you don't know what you want how can you select or ask? Guy sometimes came down after a gig with a Becks or two. It was his practice to divide his months into a two week period when he could consume alcoholic drinks and two weeks off. He never drank to excess anyway whether it was alcohol or Evian. In the non alcohol times his favourite was green tea at night, ice tea in the day. Right now he simply didn't want anything. He checked in on his emotion. It was a device he used to do in smaller seminars. He asked participants to turn to a partner immediately, don't select the group's glamour girl or comedian, turn to anyone and say unfiltered how you feel. It was a successful energiser, a safe way to be outrageous, to wear your mind on your sleeve. Guy looked straight in the mirror and said: " I feel lost. " It was almost a joke. The thousands of souls going home from a Bridges event shouting " I feel found" and the guy who galvanised it staring into the drinks fridge in indecision.

8

It was ridiculously early in the morning when the phone next to Guy's bed rang. Even an East Coast CEO wouldn't have a breakfast meeting at this hour. But if you haven't been to sleep you can't be woken up.
' Yeah,' drawled Guy.

' Guy. Maz. You alright? Oh god I've screwed up on the time zones again, that's it. Silly me.'

' Never say " silly me" Maz, dead vocabulary, remember?' Guy used the moment to pull himself up, his posture, his energy, his mood.

' Nothing gets past you, does it? Mr Bridges, day or night.'

' So where are you, my lo… partner?'

' Listen.'

' The Ocean?'

' Oh! You can hear it. They call it Kewarra, near Cairns. It is all going so well. A group of clients took me out today on the Barrier Reef.'

' You know better than that. Don't socialise with clients.'

' If we weren't too sophisticated to indulge in such clichés I'd say you got out of the wrong side of the bed this morning. Do you want to process it?'

' I haven't been to bed.'

' God, these East Coast girls…' There was a smile, a levity in Maz's voice. It suited her, thought Guy belatedly. He was trying to get his own voice up but knew he was simply coming across as short.

' I mean, I haven't been to sleep.'

Maz to her credit thought she would describe the colours of the reef some other time.

9

' What da Funk!'
Ax looked out again from the wings of the Hollywood Bowl They had never done anything this big before. Would they ever again? Ax anchored with her thoughts. She was surprised to register the feeling she was associating with Funk was bravery. She had thought many things about Funk before. Bravery wasn't one of them. Chutzpah, nerve as in cheek, conceit as in swagger but not straight full on bravery. Right there alone in the middle of the stage was Funky. Dressed all in black, still, absorbing applause. He even took his beret off to salute the crowd. All this had taken planning and nerve. Ax and Martine had really made it happen. Giving good phone, a blizzard of emails and faxes, calling in favours. Funky had said what he wanted then returned to the swirl of the Jacuzzis to enjoy the present time. Ax didn't mind. The trust was a high compliment and working with Martine wasn't always work. Ax felt proud of what she had achieved.

The tone seemed appropriate. One of the strengths of the Funk/ Ax axis had always been instinctively knowing about being just on the right side of being over the top. This wasn't a rock concert, a prayer meeting, a political rally although it was informed by aspects of those genres. When the breeze was strong enough to straighten out the multi-coloured banners you could read:

" Hard Funk: In Your State."

On a mega electronic plasma screen sponsored by a national PC supplier slogans rippled:

" Funky doesn't care if you don't."

The rocky world music band which was in the role of support act or warmer had closed their set with their anthem " No Excuses." Then Funky strolled out, a speck picked up by the cameras and relayed on to the mega screens.
It seemed an age before he spoke. Ax worried he'd finally lost it. He'd been living pretty hard on the West Coast. Ax knew about Funk's strengths, but in every strength there is a weakness. The point when playing big means going over the top, when expanding yourself means going too far, when expanding others means being obnoxious. Just as Ax began to think Funk would implode, that he really was just a speck, it began to happen.

' I'm not going to thank you for coming, we are not here to play games. You will all leave here today as different people. You are all liars, frauds, you live behind a front. Is there any one here who will challenge my assumption?'

Funky stood now on the very edge of the stage. Lights, TV and web cameras in his face. Ax began the timing. Surely it was impossible to hold this cavernous place for five minutes. Time seemed to warp, a universe in which each minute is an hour.
It was uncanny, the crowd so big behaving like an individual. At last Ax nodded to Funk. He raised his arms to the crowd – that enfolding gesture Dubcek gave the crowd from the Prague balcony after the iron curtain rose. It was exactly the right thing to do. Again Ax marvelled at how far he – they - had come.

'Give your self a round of applause, L A' said Funk before stepping back into his Hard Caring mode. He began to repeat as if to himself ' there are no excuses, there are no excuses, there can be no excuses.' The crowd picked it up, it grew into a chant. It was mesmeric. Funky began an intimate dialogue with the huge crowd, asking them questions receiving responses gospel style.

'Who is responsible for you?'
'I am responsible for myself.'
'Who is your own advocate?'
'I put myself forward.'
'Whose path do you follow?'
'I follow my own path.'

Funky knew exactly what to do. Timing, how much to share, who to invite on stage and for how long, when to lead. The time came.

'I want you all to stand up, to stand tall, to embrace the brothers and sisters around you, embrace your new life, your big life, your lie-less life. Now walk. Go.'
The band started up again "No Excuses." A single powerful firework climbed into the sky. The speck disappeared from the stage, embraced Ax, then Martine in the wings, and was gone.

10

Maz related the whole LA saga to Guy the way Ax had so excitedly and openly relayed it to her.

'Extraordinary,' repeated Guy, ' extraordinary.'

IV

1

Maz was having the time of her life. The whole post 208 trajectory had been up. Learning, doing, being, flying. Floating above the barrier reef she knew this is what she had always wanted and she wasn't going back. Back geographically maybe. But not to what she was before – a follower. She had made herself a player. She remembered how it all began, her journey from there to here and her promise to become indispensable, when the time showed itself. Maz thrived on admiration. In the past the admiration was exterior. Her posture, voice, dress sense, and it had to be said, her figure. She was imposing, a class act. In her work now all these factors were huge assets, the exterior blending with the interior. In her seminars her posture gave her authority, stillness, control. Her voice was authoritative and reassuring. Participants thought subliminally " I could be like you." Now she was being recognised intellectually and spiritually. In herself she had grown intensely in confidence, self-belief, her ambition to give.
Her progress along the coast of Australia was almost regal. Melbourne, Sydney, Brisbane, Cairns, Sydney. The pattern, the content was the same. She remained faithful to the essence of the Bridges model, using the material he had devised and they had

modified, performing under the Bridges logo and imprimatur. On the balcony of her hotel, the evening before her final engagements she re-read her journal.

' How do I feel? Proud of my achievements, my decisions, my journey, yes. In giving to others I give to myself. I feel filled up, I used to feel hollow. I have seen damaged, unwhole people change. Everything is for the better. Doubts? I admit to one. The future to resolve, my path from here. Soon I will be flying back, true, but I am not going back to my old life. The time is coming for me to fly. I will not be an employee, I will not perform under anyone's logo, I choose to be equal and free.'

She closed the journal. Sleep came gradually. Eight hours later the bedside telephone rang as arranged.
' Sydney Talk Radio. Your complimentary car will be with you in one hour. We look forward to welcoming you to our studios.'
Maz enjoyed her solitude at breakfast, feasting on the fresh fruit. She breathed deeply, released slowly silently repeating:

' Today will be a positive day, an abundant day.'

Maz swept past the hotel desk towards the chauffeur's car parked just beyond the lobby.

'Excuse me, Miss Khalm.' The hotel manager intercepted her, discreetly but forcibly.
' There seems to be a problem with the settlement of your account.'

' There must be some mistake,' she heard herself say, one of those dead lines often heard in films you never expect to say yourself. The account for each of Maz's hotels was always paid so efficiently through Guy's London accountant. The chauffeur waiting for Maz froze in the way butlers or chauffeurs do, equating keeping still with showing they were not overhearing.
The hotel manager held her ground. There wasn't a mistake. The account for Maz had been closed. It would be a positive, abundant day.

2

Success didn't change Funky. It simply enabled him to continue to be himself. The journey of Funky from leader of some indefinable London scene to an intercontinental guru was a natural progression. He had always had attention without seeking it. The attention of the media now was only new in its intensity. He welcomed it without analysis. Media attention was only a form of affirmation, a way of life. What was new for Funky, as it seemed for Maz, is that he had become a giver. It wasn't something he consciously set out to do but the combination of giving to others, to strangers, to making lives tangibly better, while making money and receiving acclaim appealed to his character. Ax had been surprised at Funky's bravery during the Hollywood Bowl extravaganza. Funk wouldn't see it that way. What was there to be brave about? He was centre stage, he was putting on a show, he was receiving attention, acclaim, giving out energy and making a difference. The attendant income boost was part of the deal. For making that amount of impact you received that amount of money. Being centre stage, being number one was part of the world order. And, Ax observed, a giving, number one Funky was just that fraction nicer to be around.

The jet was dumped at LAX. It was time for a break, some R& R after all that giving out. An Ax-less Funky boarded a scheduled flight to a Caribbean hub, then he was propelled onto St Barts. Ax and Martine headed for the hills to plan the next stages of the Funk enterprise. Pools all round. As arranged, at St Barts Funky met up again with Natasha Lake.

' Been a while, Lake darling, I missed you.' said Funk, giving her a hug.

' True. I missed you. I'm here now. Let's enjoy being together. Don't know how long we've got,' responded Lake between kisses.

It was true Funky had missed Natasha Lake. She had a wonderful presence. Her effect on Funky was brilliant, unique, giving him a centre, steadying him without any compromise on her part or character dulling constriction on his.

' Welcome, mirror woman,' he said, hugging her again.

As the mini bus rolled off to take them to lunch at Nikki Beach they sat close to each other, catching up.

' It's beautiful here,' she said simply.

' Beauty, yes, the subject of your book, the subject of you.'

Lake laughed. ' Come on Funk, you can do better than that.'

' It's true. Beauty is your thing. You are beautiful, you write about beauty, you move beautifully, you move in beautiful circles.'

' Meaning?'

' Meaning I love you. That's it. I don't have to give you a viva.'

They had an ease together. It had held, despite being apart, despite the things that happened when they were apart.

' Hey,' she said, 'I wanted to quote you this extract from an article I read on the plane.

" Let there be spaces in your togetherness,
  And let the winds of the heavens dance between you."'

' It's beautiful,' responded Funky. His eyes focussed on the middle distance. For a second he wondered how Jacuzzis with literati figured in the scheme of things. For a second, before his short term memory auto-clicked delete.

' You wrote that?'

She gave him the reference with the accuracy of an Oxford don. The Prophet. Gibran.

' Yes, it is beautiful. Perhaps it applies to us. To our future. Well, after lunch onwards.' Funky smiled and hugged her again. He loved that combination of real seriousness, of learning, levened with wit and fun. Unbelievable. ' I'll tell you something I read a few years back when I was starting out in this self-development lark.'

'You mean you read a book?'

Funky made a mock angry face then broke into a grin again.

' "There is no future, just a perpetual present". Makes us all happier.' Funk was not so scrupulous about giving sources. Bridges, first book.

' Very profound. Did you yell that out at the Hollywood bowl, Mr Development man?'

' Nope.'

' So what did you tell them, the multitude awaiting wisdom? Sometimes I wonder if the epithets you self-development guys come up with are the wisest thing since Pascal or merely on a par with the slips you find inside Christmas crackers.'

' Not merely about anything. I just told 'em how much I miss you.' It was true, really true.

' Well, we're together now. Two whole weeks. No excuses.'

The mini bus turned into the bay. Lake wound down the window, her beautiful sleek hair instantly taken up by the slipstream. A visual, auditory and olefactory sensory heaven engulfed them.

3

Natasha " Nash" Lake was as successful in her field as either Funky or Guy but she played it in a different way. The Beauty Mirror had created almost as great a stir as illustrious predecessors, even including The Female Eunuch. In many ways her position was closer to Guy's than to Funky. Her key concept was listening. Who is listened to, who is heard, how long, how deeply. Is there a connection between image and listening? Is there a link between beauty and serious attention? Lake was positioned in the public image as a serious academic and was thus exempt from the worst excesses of the paparazzi. She was a fascinating person. Her main work was in the leading universities in the UK with associate professor status in, at the last count, three Ivy League institutions in the USA. Following the publication of her book invitations to appear on radio and TV arts channels flowed freely. Incidentally, if she was concerned to check these things, she would find The Beauty Mirror currently number three behind Funky and Bridges in the US bestseller lists and number three behind Bridges and Funky in the UK. She had managed her career beautifully. Lake was seen or heard only on serious programmes, infotainment and lower was shunned. It was because that was what she wanted. Lake was totally authentic. The combination of beauty and authenticity was very powerful. To some it was frightening, others highly attractive. If you were secure yourself, and successful in your own field, like Funky, it could be a complementary power. On radio admiring listeners often found themselves quoting Shakespeare:

"Her voice was low and mellow.
Something beautiful in woman."

On TV her trademark had become her incredible composure. She remained still, often surrounded by gangs of male pundits of varying authenticity, even in the most heated of exchanges. The most excitable, and exciting gesture, she let slip was that toss of the mane of glossy black hair. At first almost imperceptible, a gesture that became slightly more emphatic in ratio to the heat of the argument. Stillness, listening, beauty. Striking, that was the adjective so often preceeding her name.
"On the panel this evening the striking academic, Dr Natasha Lake."

If she had left studio 7 with Bridges it would have been in the press next day.

" Britain's number one personal development expert leaves TV set with the striking academic. Is this a match made in heaven?"

Yet what was so striking is not only had she left the studio with Funky, gone with him to the USA and now to the Caribbean but that no one, including themselves or Ax or Maz had ever remarked on it. Guy had barely remarked on it, he had noticed it.

4

' This is WKNYAO International Boston. We welcome this morning, from London, England, Guy Bridges. Welcome Guy, thanks for swinging by.'

' It's a pleasure to be here,' replied Guy, a smile in his voice.

Guy was doubt-free again. Restored by sleep, prayer, the continued acclaim from the East Coast audiences, by reasoned praise from Louisa-May. Wherever the ripple of doubt in Baltimore had come from it had now dissipated. As a leader Guy of course continually analysed his situation. The Baltimore Dip as his self talk came to refer to it was possibly a combination of road fatigue, of too many beige hotels, an untimely, unsettling call from Maz and the presence of that coutured woman in the second row which he had difficulty ascertaining as positive, neutral or negative. He followed his own teachings. After analysis, put your thoughts on the back burner, solutions, feelings will emerge. Trust the path, trust your self, and ultimately follow your inner voice over the chatter of external rationalisings. Guy had a series of inner chants, sayings he had offered in his book for reorientating yourself, rescuing remedies for doubt, fear of not being good enough, of being rumbled. Feedback told him it was one of the most appreciated parts of his latest book. People were surprised at how quickly they could be turned round using these techniques, chants, inner prayers, self-talk.

You could repeat these sayings in absolutely any situation. Going into a job interview, meeting a potential partner, asking for a change, or if you were just a man from Leeds about to go on a prestige high profile radio show with your reputation on the line. If your inner voice always said " I'm lost" simply repeat " I know the way."
If the little voice insinuated " I'm not good enough" repeat " I can excel in whatever comes my way." Refocus the belief " I am a skill-less imposter" with the affirmation " I have, have had and always will have the power within me."

' WKNYAO. This is Lenny's Life Line. Before we open up to our callers. Tell us something about yourself Guy. Maybe most of our listeners will know you already. Tell us something new.'

' Bowl away, Lenny.'

' I love it bowl away, bowl away. Nicely lobbed back. What a pro. Nice to work with the best. OK, Let me send this down to you. If you weren't the world's leading self development guru…'

' Facilitator, trainer, presenter…'

' What?'

' Guru, not a word I use.'

' With you, Guy. If you weren't the world's leading however you want to describe your self what would you be doing right now?'

' I don't know. I am doing what I'm doing right now.'

' If?'

' I don't work in ifs. What use is it to do that?'

' Let me quote a fact at you Guy, we'll drop the ifs. Here it is. A striking Ivy League academic, Dr Natasha Lake, wrote a review of a series of your seminars. The average attendance rates at your events is generally around 80% women. It's a fact. How would you explain that, Guy?'

' How did Lake explain it? I only offer my seminars in a spirit of service. If only one person came I would consider that a success. It's a honour to do what I do.'

' Dr Lake wrote about listening. Your work is highly centred on the skill of listening. Some other gurus out there, that Funky fella is one example, work in a different way, a more aggressive way, may I say a more masculine way. Open question: do you believe there is a masculine or feminine way to work in your field, are there gender characteristics?'

' Lenny, every time you try and make a rule, all women are, all men are, you are going to get deluged with exceptions, with stories, histories. I do what I do. I'm a man. Funky does what he does. He's a man. There are others. They do what they do. Some men are radio presenters, carpenters, drug dealers, pianists. They do what they do. I don't analyse that. I do it. I aim to help others help themselves. If I help one person it's all worthwhile.'

' Nice line Guy. And the lines of WKNYAO are buzzing too. Who's Life is on the Line to Guy Bridges?'

' Hi Guy. It's Lorraine from Hartford. I love your seminars. My life has changed so much so quickly. But for you Guy, as my kind of mentor, I would be interested to know what do you think are the most important principles to live by?'

' Hi Lorraine,' responded Guy, entering into the swing of it all, ' thanks for swinging by my seminars.' Swinging by? When had he ever said that before he asked himself? Must have been away from home too long. 'To me the key word is authenticity. Be yourself, trust yourself, then nothing can go wrong, everything will come right. Lead you own life, not the life other people expect or want you to leave, the life people would be scared if you lived in another way. Be your own wonderful self.'

' That is so beautiful Guy. And practical. Thank you.'

' WKNYAO. Who is next on the life line live to Guy Bridges?'

Lenny took more short calls, equal numbers from men and women. Many had attended Guy's gigs on the East Coast, compliments flowed, genuine not gushing. Guy was gracious without being anodyne. It was good live radio but Lenny wanted to spice things up.

' Guy, how can I become more confident?'

' That is so interesting,' said Lenny.' Can you give us your name and let's see if Guy can fix your confidence right here on WKNYAO.'

' I am Francoise.'

' She's all yours Guy.'

' Thanks, Lenny. Tell us more Francoise. Do you have any reason not to be confident?'

' I am a successful business woman. I live a sham. I hate myself. I have so much money, I have nothing, I am nothing...'

Guy tried to lighten things up a fraction. 'That's quite a list. How long is this prog, Len?'

' Long enough Guy, long enough.'

' Why don't you help me Guy? You can't or you won't?'

Guy took a deep breath. He had this desire to tell the woman to sod off. The voice was ever so vaguely familiar, or may be it was just a type. Her English was on the dead side of perfect. She thought fooling around with grammar was intrinsically interesting. He tried to keep the edge out of his voice. Radio could wreck you up as easily and as quickly as TV. Guy had a flash image of a test batsman accumulating a crucial century: takes skill, patience, flair but you could be out any moment, floundering, embarrassed. Guy recommenced his technique of asking questions back.

' Do you have any reason not to be confident, Francoise?'

' You aren't taking this seriously,' she said with an intonation difficult to place.

' I only want to be more confident. I would give all my wealth to be confident.'

' I believe you are confident now Francoise. I believe it. You can believe it too. There was a time too when you believed you were confident. You were born confident you just left it behind somewhere along the road, like a parcel. Why don't you just reopen it? What's the payoff? Do you enjoy not being confident? Are you worried other people may not like you any more if you are confident? You can do anything you want. You can make money, you can give it away, you have travelled to where you are now. No one can take away your good feelings about yourself. You can be whoever you are. You can just decide to be a confident person.
Just repeat that after me. I am confident. I decide to be confident. I decide now. Picture yourself being weak and defeated. Now picture yourself standing tall and confident. Which would you rather be? Just take a deep breath and decide.'

There was a silence. Lenny let it run. His producer was just about to cut in when they all heard sobbing on the line.

' I... I decide to be whoever I am...I'

Guy felt better. The " sod you" feeling melted down. He'd engaged.

' Say it again Francoise. Say it, believe it, be it. What have you got to lose? What is the payoff about staying where you are? What is so great about not being confident that you feel like you want to continue to be like that? The unconfident you is finished. Take a deep breath, smile, decide, I am reaching out with a beautiful big box of confidence for you. Open it. It's yours. You deserve it. Decide. Decide, say it, I decide to be confident. I am so confident I never even think about it.'

The pause continued again. Then a loud, almost unrecognizable voice came back over the airwaves.

' I Francoise decide to be confident. I have decided not to continue with the old me. I have opened a lovely box of confidence.' Her voice rang off Lenny's programme like a peal of bells on a May morning. ' I love being confident....'

' Wow,' said Lenny, ' that was really something. That was world class, Mr Bridges. We're going to take one more call on this WKNYAO special. Let's go out on a real high. That's going to be a hard act to follow. Who's on the line caller?'

' It's Maz from Sydney. Where's my money Bridges you snakey bastard?'

5

To say that Maz was similar to the lead character in Mary Shelley's Frankenstein was unfair and at least visually, misleading. The pact freely entered into in room 208 was two way. Guy was top of his field but needed new input and stimulation, a foil. If you do what you've always done, you'll get what you always get. Guy got success but although he probably didn't really know it, was treading water. In this field you can receive new input through material, through reading, through osmosis. You can also simply be moved forward by coming across new, unusual people, and in this case coming across new unusual people in an unusual way. Initially it is true Maz learned the most, had the most to learn and the most to gain. She was learning from Guy. Guy gave freely. His belief that giving freely without thought of return was also a form of giving to yourself was vindicated. Maz did not give him new material in the conventional sense. The written material given out at seminars or disseminated through the web was Guy's. An academic may of course ask where did Guy derive the material from? The originality is in the mix, the slant, and in the delivery. In this way Maz toured Australia under her own colours almost as much as Guy's. But she stuck to the pact, intending to fly solo after a discussion and thank you to Guy in London.

Email, fax, voice mail, and late night intercontinental telephone conversations are all ways of keeping in touch but Guy and Maz had not actually seen each other for over a month. Ax gave better phone than Guy. Maz could visualize Funky out there more vividly than Guy. The beret, the strut, the catchphrase, the no-nonsense bullshit. Guy was more like a spirit, able to walk on water and through walls but difficult to imagine. Resentments, real or imagined bubbled up. All very lower self but what are you supposed to do with the shadow side? Guy never initiated communication with Maz. It was always her who looked at her cube clock, calculated time zones with an accuracy in ratio to her mood and made the call. Out there on the antipodean stages she caught herself frowning at the Guy Bridges logos and web name. All apparently minor but the feeling persisted and niggled on both sides that one was giving more than the other despite deployment of techniques intended to dispel it.

Maz thought about the situation emotionally. Guy when he thought about it at all thought practically. Time zones can be a real bummer. Not only are you ringing your correspondent when they are in a different zone of time, on a different bio-rhythm, they are going to be in a different bubble. Just getting up, just going to sleep, just starting a great day or finishing a real belter. Guy had even counseled people about telephones earlier in his career. Telephone calls between couples, even in the same time zone were difficult enough. Mobiles often seemed to loom up as real problem makers.
Guy gave out this rule. Don't make a mobile call that you wouldn't bother to go to a pay phone to make. Then of course he broke it. Another of these endless hotels, the beige, the small hours, that lethal mix. He called Maz in Sydney. Didn't even try to work out the time zone side of things. She didn't pick up. The gist of the message he left was time for Maz to fly. This included the financial side of things. His organisation would no longer be paying hotel bills. All the training and seminar fees would go directly to her bank account in London. She was free to work under her own name and logos. Starting now. In a blitz of messaging he emailed his London accountant on the laptop to put the process in motion. In the morning he woke with a start, opened his email to stop the wheels turning. Before he could activate his send box the inbox pinged with the confirmation from his ever efficient accounts manager.

' Re Maz: Sydney hotel payments stopped with immediate effect as requested.'

Guy ruefully made a note in his journal:

' some clichés are true, act in haste, repent at leisure. Sleep on it. They sound too unsophisticated to us professionals. But it is just a different language.'

Then he started a new page. Under the heading Maz, he wrote:

'What do I really think about her?' Then divided the page into columns headed work play sex past present future, switched the pen into his other hand and began to write with a stream of consciousness flow.

6

From Past It by Guy Bridges:

' All of you isn't all the same all of the time. As an individual you can move from full higher self to the lowest of lower self in an instant. But it is still you, who you are. It is simply important that you know about it. Nod or smile to your self in recognition. Self talk yourself up to where you want to be, to where you envisage yourself. If you are slumped, fed up, out of sorts whatever the name you give to such a state simply say do I want to look like this, sound like this, come across like this? Decide. No one has time to waste being down but you can be sure it will happen. It's only the flip side to being up. It's all still you. If, or to be more exact when, you find yourself in a low mood, simply say hello friend, smile, and pull over and let it pass. It's just a lorry load of thoughts. Lorries can carry anything from beautiful loads of fresh exotic fruit to rolls of barbed wire. They can easily be unloaded and refilled. Pull over and let them pass. They will be happy to and you will be happy too. You can choose what you think about, what you dwell on, what state you want to operate in. What load would you rather be carrying? A negative you is only that happy, positive person you are naturally, thinking you are in a negative mood. Nothing externally has changed. Have you ever touched a mood? Let it pass and reload with abundance.'

The book did not explicitly cover going on radio in low moods.

7

Their talk shows, or as Guy and Maz described them in the tour planning – wireless showcase – were mirror images. Guy went onto his show in Boston a few hours after unleashing the infamous Maz message, Maz was on 'Sydney, Let's Talk' an hour after being informed by the Four Seasons concierge there was a problem. She strode into the studio, her anger slightly subsiding but still at an enjoyably high level. The car ride from the hotel to the studio gave Maz enough of a buffer zone to adjust her mind set to self talk herself higher.

" A week, a month, a year from now none of this will matter."
" I am loving the message, the learning in this."
" Everything is happening for a higher purpose."

All elementary chapter one stuff but it seemed to be working enough for Maz to manage her anger and continue to function as people now expected her to. She had billed this wireless showcase to herself as simultaneously the last gig under the Bridges umbrella and her first one totally under her own auspices. She had after all calmed down enough to know that the Bridges logo had got her to this point, the back of a studio bound limo in Sydney, or at the very least propelled her to these heights in this period of time. Completely solo from day one it would have taken years. But that's it, all fulfilled, the apogee of project 208. This show, fly back to London, regroup, relaunch.

The presenter was a young trendy Sydneysider operating under the name of Zak. His head was shaved and shiny, a pair of Gucci shades permanently worn on his pate despite his operational world being a windowless bunker. The look, coupled with a manner so breezy it was aggressive added irritation on top of Maz's only slowly receding anger. Guy's image came clearly into her head. She preferred the way Guy looked much more than all of these younger media men she had come across on her itinerary since Rotterdam. He even had a parting, for God's sake. The shiny shoes, he was really such a decent sort she mused, as the anger clouds dissipated. Whatever happened, whatever she planned next she had learned so much, come so far, and hoped they would always be… friends.

' Hey, Maz, you up for this?' shot Zak. No pauses or reveries here Maz said to herself. The anger ebbed and flowed. " The snakey bastard, the double-dealer, all men are…" competed in her thoughts with " cruel to be kind, what did you expect, you got what you wanted, girl."

' We're on in one,' continued Zak. 'We'll do it as we agreed with your office. Coupla warm up calls from some suburban saddos then we'll do a Lazurus.'

' A what?'

' Something for real. Get a basket case to ring in. You turn'em round, they get up and sprint away. You up for it? I seem to keep losing contact with you.'

Maz searched for a phrase that would get her back into the groove of things.

' Bring'em on,' she said, an expression totally alien to her.

Over the top of Zak's sunglasses she saw the sign light up: On Air.

Maz surfed on the combination of the remants of her anger and her aversion to Zak's communication style to find the energy and verve to do well with the warm up callers. She relaxed and began to think of her triumphant return to London, her solo future. She was on the path.
Zak smoothly set up the centre piece.

' This is Sydney Let's Talk with your own Zak and our special guest Maz from London. We don't promise miracles but you can always ask.'
Maz was becoming slightly alarmed at this Lazarus / miracle direction Zak was pushing.

' Zak, Maz. Good day. It's Frank from Darlinghurst.'

' The airwaves are yours, Frank.'

' I'd like to ask Maz this,' mumbled Frank from Darlinghurst. 'Maz, I'd like you to help me. It's simply this. I'd like to be more confident, to believe in myself, to have no issues around confidence.'

Maz began brightly. 'Do you have any reason not to be confident Frank?'

' Sometimes I'm confident, sometimes I'm not. I seem to oscillate between two extremes. Sometimes I feel like a total sham, I feel I am nothing.'

' That is only natural Frank,' rejoined Maz. ' We all oscillate, as you so clearly put it, from our higher, visible self to our lower, shadow self. Call it what you will, moods, frames of mind. They are all you. You simply need to integrate them, say hello to them both.'

' How do I do that Maz ?'

' Every one is born confident. Have you ever seen an unconfident new born babe? As time goes on we get knocked around. It's called life. We receive messages. Maybe from parents, friends, teachers, even from radio and TV. Underneath it all there is the real, original, confident Frank. You simply have to choose. Think about it. There is no reason not to be confident. It's your natural state. Choose. It's all there for you just the same as it is for us all. Look in a mirror. See yourself. Smiling, standing tall, welcoming to yourself, to people around you at work, family, friends. Take a deep breath and decide Frank. Let's do it together. Say after me. I Frank, decide now to be confident, to enjoy life, there is every reason to do so. Over to you Frank.'

There was a silence, infinitesimal in terms of the Universe, an age in terms of Let's Talk Sydney. Eventually Frank came through.

' I… I … Frank decide to be con…' He fizzled out.

Maz lowered her voice a tone and continued. ' We're with you Frank. You're nearly there. Just decide. Be confident. It is your right to be confident. Take it. Be it. Say it.'

The silence began again. Zak's sunglasses came down from his forehead to his eyes like a knight lowering a visor. Maz knew he'd received a message from the producer. Zak cut in.

' Maz, give the guy a hand. Help him some more. We're with you Frank.'
Maz continued in her own way. Then handed the airwaves back to Frank. The silence stuttered on. On air a weedy voice came back through the headphones to Maz, Zak and anyone else in New South Wales who was concerned with these kind of issues.

' When I was at school it was all so unfair…'

She looked straight back into Zak's shades. It all happened in a fraction. She could see Zak about to cut the mike, a failure, her failure, her tour would end like this. A radio producer using a commercial break to fill silence. It wasn't even her material. It was bloody Bridges who wasn't working. Working for her. Zak was now making a piratical cut gesture across his throat. She suddenly heard a voice, it didn't even sound like her, almost shouting in the microphone.

' Frank. I want you to stand up. Now at home. You are going to say right now to me, Zak, everyone in Sydney. I am confident. The game is up Frank and any other losers, pretenders, evaders who are eavesdropping. We are sick of your excuses, you feeling sorry for yourself. I don't care why it is, who it was, or how you've got to where you are. The past is gone. Your old life, your life of excuses is over. There is only the present, and everything waiting for you in the future if you chose it. Get over yourself, quit whingeing and damn well say it. I am confident. I choose this way.'

Her voice was hard, strident. Zak even had his sunglasses off to look at her. She was about to launch into a tirade against the blasted invisible miserable bastard of a Frank when it came through strongly.

' I'm Frank, I'm confident, course I am, I bloody well am.'

He could feel the change coming through the radio. Sounds seemed to indicate Frank had stood up in some epiphanic moment and was embracing anyone near him. Maz was standing too in the studio, shaking, staring into the middle distance. Zak seemed about to say something profound. Instead he merely said

' We'll be right back after this' and slid up the control levers to the sounds of some easy listening sludge. They never did come right back.

8

Hours later high over the Indian Ocean Maz was dreaming.

By the Caribbean Funky was massaging coconut oil into Lake's cleavage outwards in a clockwise motion.

By the Pacific Ax was massaging coconut oil into Martine's back outwards in an anti-clockwise motion.

High over the Atlantic en route to Paris Francoise was flicking the airline movie channel.

High over the Atlantic en route to London Guy was writing in his journal:

' I am always learning. I am always learning. I am always learning.'

WISE GUY…

V

1

' What the Funk, that's…..emmm,' sighed Lake above her oiled glistening breasts. That is so b…'

' Beautiful,' laughed Funk and Lake together.

They had become closer on the island. Funky seemed mellower than in London. Lake called it location specific. People emphasise different character traits in different locations. Once Funky even referred to Guy Bridges in a non-aggressive manner. Talked about having him come over to the new centre. She hadn't quite understood at the time. Did it mean a centre, a place or to be centred, guru- speak. Lake didn't pursue it because she didn't want Funky to be always talking about other people and places when they were together right here, right now. Like all couples they had their private jokes and ceremonies. Natasha was always called Lake. Funky was always called Funk. Funky liked to tease Lake about using the word beauty like Mark Anthony used the word honourable. Lake seemed to be in a kind of swoon, her voice descending lower and lower.

' I wish we didn't ever have to go back,' she said.

' We're not,' replied Funky.

' We are not going back? You mean ever?'

' You've got it Lake. I don't think about going back. Too conceptual. We are going to stay here in this perpetual present. Everything is going to come to us. Everything we need that isn't already here.'

' Another plan to take over the world?'

' If that's what the world wants. Welcome to The Healing Beach. We are going to heal the world right here from this beach. A new centre. Courses, group work, spa, you name it. We are going to make it happen. The centre is here. The world will come to us.'

' The Healing Beach?'

' Yeah, it's going to be so b…'

' Beautiful,' they exclaimed together.

Funky outlined his plans in a drawl that for him passed as excitement.
' I'm gonna call Ax right now. She'll have to run the London end, the business shit.'

Funk stood up, his eyes looking out to sea, the vision already becoming real. He was about to swap the coconut oil bottle for the mobile. Lake put her hand over his and drew him back to the present.

' Funk,' she said.

' Lake?'

' Don't stop.'

2

From Heathrow Guy took the Airbus directly to his Holland Park house. Within hours of arriving home he fell into a deep sleep. The tour was a great success but not without strains.

Guy's work meant giving. Giving out energy, engaging with people who were at least initially energy drains, requiring thought, imagination, engagement to turn around. Not only had he given out energy all along the east coast of the USA, he'd given out energy to Maz. The idea that Maz might be his creation never occurred to Guy. It wasn't the sort of thought he entertained. Not now, in this present. He was happy to give and it wasn't all one way. To give without thought for what may be returned to you is also a form of receiving. Energy simply circulates. People can learn from you and then they fly in their own way. You can't make anything happen that isn't supposed to. Everyone is always learning therefore everyone is always changing. That's the only constant.

Guy slept and slept. He woke up, smiled at the sky and began to think about what he would do next. Then he remembered Maz. Was it what he would do next or what they would do next? Or both? Guy was well aware of the dynamics of the work he did. The need to recharge after all that giving out. Sleep, high fruit diet, living in your own space were all part of it. He enjoyed his time after a period of intense work. Guy was able to thrive for long though not excessive periods of time in his own company. Never mawkish or lost, but peaceful, self-contained moving at his own pace. He read, wrote his journal, meditated. His technical people attended to the Guy Bridges web site but he responded dutifully to their emails as required. There was an empire to run and it had his name on it. His admin people in London and Louisa – May in the USA filtered his calls. He regularly checked his answer-phone and voice mail for calls allowed through. Most mornings there were calls from journalists, the occasional
Ph D student, a select coterie of fellow professionals he compared ethical notes with as a safety peer mentoring procedure. He realised after a few days when he went to his answer machines he was really checking for messages from Maz. There weren't any. Maybe she was recuperating too he half thought. The other half of the thoughts, the real half, knew he was being ignored, snubbed even. Despite himself, the non-communication from his erstwhile mentee, partner and now peer irked him. Right from 208 there was something about Maz he could never place. Never place about himself. Though technically he had given to Maz, he seemed to have the feeling he wanted something from her. Sex. Recognition. Gratitude? For her to depend on him?
It irked him he couldn't ever figure it out completely. He back-burnered it. The answer would present itself.

On one of these compulsive phone checking sessions there was a message from Toby, TV producer and tennis partner.
' Guy, hear you transformed the East Coast. Pity you can't do anything about that backhand of yours.'

' Toby, is this a business or social call?'

' I'm very well too Guy, thank you. Actually it's both. How about we meet at the club, I smash you love all and then we have a natter about a show I'm putting together? See you at 12 as usual. Tomorrow?'

' Show?'

' You know better than to mess around with words Guy. We all do shows now. I think the Third Programme went off air a while back. Are we on?'

' 12 it is, Tobe.'

' Until tomorrow,' said Toby.

Guy enjoyed the day and slept well, although a faint sense, not of forboding, but of something about to happen began to pervade. Guy hated any kind of new age stuff, astrology, crystals and showed his disdain if anyone around him personally or professionally mentioned it. Charlatans all. He did believe however in critical points, opportunities, seizing the time present in those intersections. Things happen for a reason. Things manifesting for a negative reason, such as neglect, or a positive reason, because you've made a decision, you've put out for something.
This feeling Guy had wasn't big and it wasn't rational. The only time he had even slightly felt this before was when he could feel his temper rising on that US talk programme. A feeling he was just a word away from blowing everything he was. It was there, following him along the bike lane on his way to the tennis club the next morning. The set with Toby had become absurd. In the final game they moved quickly to deuce. Then advantage Guy, back, advantage Toby, back. It went on forever. By the 8th back to deuce Toby mid game clearly offered an honourable draw. Guy simply slammed the ball back over the net twice.

' Everything alright, old fruit?' asked Toby in the club house dining area.

' Fine,' said Guy, ' fine,' waving his hand palm down in a " this line is closed before it starts" gesture.

Over the Caesar salads Toby moved on to business.
' This is the format. We live in a world obsessed with celebs, idols…'

' We do?'

' Will you stop pratting about with this innocent act, Guy. Where is all this stuff coming from?'

' What stuff?'

' You are as much as a celeb as any one else. An anti–celeb is still a celeb. Best seller lists, talk-ins, trans-Atlantic heal-ins.'

' It has taken me years to get to where I am. There is content in my work.'

' Didn't say there wasn't, old fruit. You need the media as much as we need you. Can we continue?'

Guy peered into the salad. The ratio of chicken to lettuce was irritating. He took a deep breath and looked back steadily at Toby.
Toby continued his pitch. ' Guy, you pioneered the movement of self development, mind-body-spirit work, call it what you will, from obscure flakedom to the centre stage of our world. You are number one in the best seller lists…'

' In the UK and Europe.'

' In the UK and Continental Europe, quite, and have just returned from a US biggy. Next step? You are at the top Guy. You want to stay there. You have so much to give. You have so many strengths and skills, you are a kind of celeb, but you are real, authentic, anti-flash. Almost, I say this positively, from a bygone age. In TV terms the pre-celeb, reality TV age. It is part of your USP. So this is it. I think, though I say it myself, it's a genius idea, simple yet universal. Celebrity Turnaround. We are going to take the biggest, most messed up celebs in the world and you Guy are going to turn 'em around on prime time TV.'

Guy looked at Toby almost expecting him to light a Groucho Marx style cigar.
' No.'

They returned to deuce. Advantages of doing or not doing the project were played over the table. At the close of the lunch the two retired to the terrace with their Earl Grey. Guy realised he was coming across as prim, even antediluvian. Toby was totally correct. Guy was a media figure, a star himself. Maybe he didn't desport himself before Saints Barts or Tropez but that was simply his choice. In essence the only new point about Toby's proposal was that Guy would be working one to one with selected celebs rather than " ordinary" people who self–selected themselves to come along to his events. Stars were people too. Really they were simply people like Guy, people at the top of their chosen field. Besides, what was next for him? Louisa –May had told him about the rumours of Funky's island Healing Beach. Guy had rested enough. To tread water was to sink. His objections evaporated.
' Yes.'

3

Guy returned to his routine with purpose. Reading, writing, appointments with long standing private clients. Many of these clients were celebrities. Considering Guy's hourly rate they had to be, although Guy did have a sliding scale so that he could still work with genuine cases of reduced financial means. The London office and Louisa-May kept him in touch with business developments. He'd instructed Toby's broadcasting company to work through the London office though he understood celebs for the grill, as Toby's people rather alarmingly called the project, could be from the UK, USA or EU countries. Guy was calm and productive though he still occasionally awoke with that feeling, what he by now had nick-named The Cloud.

The fax arrived the day before the first show was due on air. Toby had negotiated syndication rights for the format on the basis of Guy's reputation and on the quality of the celebs to be lined up. The show was to broadcast live in the UK. A company called Du Pont Broadcasting would operate the European distribution and there would be re-broadcasting in the US. It was a huge deal. Guy felt pleased and skimmed over the big print of the fax. Small print wasn't for him to deal with. He was the product.

Guy had spent his time well. He never forgave himself if he wasted time, let it slip away for nothing. He applied himself to the project. What did he really understand about celebrity culture, what was the thread? At the heart of Guy's teaching was the belief in authenticity. It wasn't an original concept. Guy drew on hypnotherapy, psychotherapy and other disciplines but he made everything his own. Others in his field had long talked about the higher self, source, an essence. Some gave this a religious base – Christian, Buddha, whatever source or tradition they chose. Others simply call the source love. When we are cut off or cut ourselves off from this love, this source we become inauthentic. We are playing a role. A role we may have decided to play or think others will be pleased or placated if we play it. Because we are living a role we live in fear, or is that hope, we will be discovered. Time passes, layers are built over the original source, the you. Guy thought about this. The show he was about to go on was for prime time TV. So he needed to be authentic, get his ideas across quickly, without pretence but be true to himself and his work. He must have integrity. He must be trusted. He mustn't commit the ultimate TV sin, droning onto long. It is true, as Toby had to point out, that he too was a celeb but he did not live what he understood by the celeb lifestyle. In his own experience of the media he had seen some of the workings of the denizens of planet celeb. Globally famous names instructing their agents to haggle over the running order of their appearance on guest shows, tantrums over the wrong brand of mineral water in the green room. He had also seen people of talent, generosity, fun. He believed that those who were in trouble with addictions, who were run by their egos had simply lost contact with their real self. Fear and insecurity are partners. On the programme Guy would talk the guest back through the accumulated layers to what he called The Start, a point analogous to that of a new born child, for whom everything is in front of them without condition. Guy had helped so many women and men using this de-layering technique, talking back to the Start. It had never failed.

He called this the EASE programme. Encouraging Active Listening in a Supportive Environment. For many people, whoever they were, the experience of being actively listened to, 100% full on attention, was almost unprecedented in their lives. Certainly in their adult lives. This in itself was simply enough to turn people around. Guy may implant an image here, a suggestion there, but people really did it all themselves once they had the searing experience of being listened to in this way. The only problem Guy was savvy enough to foresee was it could take time and it can be met with initial resistance before people realise that to continue as they are is actually less fun then dropping the baggage of their lifetime and starting their journey again. Some friction makes for good TV. Long quivering silences don't. Guy trusted himself.

Quote from Guy's journal:

' "the spiritual path is a journey without a distance, to a place we never left."
Anonymous source.'

4

It felt good to back in studio seven. Guy felt almost at home. Toby was there, some familiar faces, a scene of past successes for Guy and, Toby hoped, for future triumphs. To push himself into big star mode Guy had ditched his morning cycle ride to the studio and come in by TV company limo. He preferred the bike. Arriving at the studio two other limos were parked on the forecourt. One the same as his, the other a stretch job as long as a train. He wondered why there were two and remembered stories he had heard, of stars demanding limos, dressing rooms or trailers of specific dimensions. The lights were as strong as ever.

' Hi Guy,' said a matter of fact voice.

Guy whirled round, at a disadvantage by having to stare directly into the white blast. The lights silhouetted Maz. He moved towards her to give her a hug. She moved towards him to give him a business style handshake. As a result the contact was fumbled. Before Guy could decide a line to take Toby was in front of them. Toby greeted Guy with an arm movement simulating a perfect serve just inside the base line which a partner would have no hope of returning. He was surrounded by assistants, like a consultant on a ward. He introduced an icily elegant woman to Guy.
' Guy. Francoise du Pont. She will be taking the show on her European channels.' Toby hadn't got to where he was in his field without being able to pick up on a frisson. 'Have you two met before?'

Guy shook hands with Francoise perfunctorily. She smiled at him. One of those instants which could say I've known you forever. He stared straight back at her. Then glanced at Maz and back to Toby.
' Toby,' said Guy. 'I thought I was doing this alone.'

He was trying not to sound rude to Maz or egotistical to Toby.
' You got the fax, old fruit. TV at this level needs a bit of spice. Miss Khalm has been making quite a stir I hear in Oz. Her approach a fraction more, shall we say confrontational than yours. Should be great live. May the best guru win.
It's Celebrity Turnaround.'

Maz was on first. She was composed, beautifully dressed, clothes and make-up colour coordinated. She had twenty minutes, including one commercial break, to turn around a rock singer. The singer was world famous, highly talented but erratic. Her albums veered between genius and vacuousness. She had tangled with drug abuse and was becoming unreliable and difficult to work with. Not in an allowably temperamental thespy way but simply tiresome. Expensive studios lying idle in her absence, projects abandoned. A bomb site of a personal life. The record companies continued with her in case another album of genius emerged. But it was well known she was on notice. She had volunteered to come on the show and was exactly the sort of tight rope walker that Toby wanted. Maz began simply.
' Why are you here ?' she said in a flat tone.

The singer seemed spaced out, alternating between aggression and lassitude.

' You are going to sort me out,' she shot back, playing to the gallery.

' That is just where you are wrong,' said Maz staying in this flat tone, her eye contact unrelenting, no trace of a smile on her lips.

The singer seemed slightly miffed at the grey carpet treatment.

' Don't you know who I am?' she began.

Maz was almost contemptuous.
' Don't you?'

The star withdrew into a kind of sulk. Toby watching from the control room feared a walkout. Walkouts can be fine but preferably after the commercial break.
Maz seemed to know exactly what to do with silent space on TV.
' I'm asking you again, why are you here?'
The star looked straight back at Maz for an age. Then looked at the studio floor and went into a confessional mode. She began a litany of what was wrong in her life. Her addiction to alcohol, various prescribed and unprescribed drugs, a life of loneliness despite never being alone, a fear of losing a talent, maybe she never even had a talent, she was a husk, afraid, didn't know what to do. She began to sob gently. Maz was so still. Eventually she said, still in her flat tone.
' And what are you going to do now?'

' I need help, you must… it isn't my fault. I need another chance…someone must be able to help me…when I was younger I…'

' No. I said what are you going to do now?'

Assistants hovered in the background of the studio. Toby had recruited some final year up to the eyeball indebted psychiatry students from the London teaching hospitals as backup. They would be paid a fairly substantial appearance fee to be on hand during the show to cover any eventualities. Their resemblance to members of Pan's People was coincidental. The studio controller moved them forward. To viewers at home they would appear as a semi-circle around the star, on the edge of the screen.
The star ceased sobbing and became belligerent.
' You think it's easy being me? Performing, delivering all the time.
I need help.'

' So you need someone else to do something for you?'

There was a stir in the studio audience. Of course part of the premiss of the show was some celeb getting their booty kicked. But the great British public also had a sense of what they believed to be fair play. Tough love was a US import.
The celeb seemed to try to out-silence Maz. This time Maz was fine with speaking first.
' Stand up. I said stand up.' The astonished singer slowly rose to her feet as if attached to a stage hoist. ' You can make a choice now. Stay as you are. Stuck with your drugs

and self indulgence and excuses. Or throw away the props and be everything you can be. Your call.'

There was a pause then Maz continued.
' Say after me. My old life, my life of excuses is over, my big life, my lie-less life starts now.'

The singer started to say the words after Maz like one half of a couple at an old fashioned wedding then began to play with the words, singing, chanting, jamming. Her face changed colour from goth white to a healthy luminescence. Her posture upright, her gaze steady.
She embraced Maz. There was an audible thank you. The audience broke into sustained applause. The singer waved.

' Fade to the break,' said Toby. ' Celebrity Turnaround is going to be big, big, big. Top that Bridges.'

5

Francoise du Pont was the biggest TV mogul in Europe. Turner, Murdoch, Du Pont. They owned the air. Guy in his other worldliness didn't know how famous she was. Her personal wealth was higher than many non G8 economies. But she had taste, style. Beautiful and elegantly dressed she was famous particularly in Continental Europe but could walk along the street in virtual anonymity in the UK or US. Guy could feel when Toby formally introduced her she was a person of power. She hadn't quite given out that kind of aura when he saw her at the US seminar. He recalled now the two things true one false intro Maz did way back in Rotterdam. The false point was that she was a TV addict. She wasn't addicted to watching TV. She was addicted to buying TV stations. Guy's head selected a song like a jukebox.
" Money can't buy you love."
Guy was number one in the UK and European bestseller lists. He remembered now seeing the name Francoise du Pont year after year at the top of the rich list. Yet she radiated aloneness. Not the aloof, separateness of successful tycoons, just someone alone. No friends, no lovers, another evening at home with nothing on TV. Thinking about it Guy remembered her from seminars he'd given all over the world. She must have flown in by private jet to take in a seminar with the same nonchalance that her consumers at home all over Europe were tuning into a show on her channels. So far away from her business operating base she could play out her problems with no danger of embarrassment to her business interests. Clever but calculating, a solution and problem at the same time.

Shrewdly Toby had asked her to be the celebrity for Guy to turnaround on this first show. For the first UK show Toby didn't want a high profile A lister. But the name Francoise du Pont was well known enough to be a ratings draw. Millions of viewers would tune in. How would she dress, what would someone who owned so many TV stations actually look like on TV? If she's so rich and business savvy why is she so messed up? How would the amazing Guy Bridges work with someone so powerful? It was a TV win –win, a showstopper. If Bridges succeeded, in the way the show's remit defined success, everyone is happy and they'd be laughing all the way to the

Monte Carlo TV awards. If Bridges didn't make Du Pont as happy as she was rich it simply meant they needed more time. Not another show, another series.
Toby was deep in the control room in a haze of self congratulation when Guy tapped him on the shoulder.
' Get back on court Guy,' ordered Toby, ' we're live in 5.'

' Toby you should know I've "done" this woman before.'

' Boasting eh, Guy. Look, old boy, this isn't the time for bedpost notching. Get on my studio floor now.'

' No, I mean on the radio.'

' I don't care if it was on the stairs Guy…'

' I mean we were on a phone-in in the States. I've already, as you might put it, turned her round.'

Guy was beginning to tire of the whole thing. Why had he agreed? He hated the expression turnaround. The cloud thickened. And Maz, where had all that come from? A voice shouted " three minutes."

' I know Guy, I know. She told me. You turned her round on radio. Turn her on – I mean turn her round on my TV show. Now get out of my face.'

10, 9, a make up assistant patted Guy's hair, 4,3, 2…

' Francoise, welcome,' began Guy in that wonderfully modulated voice of his.
' It's a pleasure to see you,' he said, deliberately omitting the word "again."
He continued. ' You've volunteered to come on this programme, Francoise. Tell us why.'

' I live a double life. I am known as a successful business woman. Materially I have everything I want. I confess to being unhappy.'

' How are you unhappy, Francoise?'

' I am lonely. I am lonely. There is no centre to my life.'

' There is no centre to my life,' said Guy, deadpan.

' Excuse me,' said Francoise, a flicker of alarm in her blue eyes.

' There is no centre to *my* life. That's it. There is no centre to my life.'

It seemed as if no one in the studio was breathing, it was so still.
Francoise gazed back at him. In one fluid movement Guy stood up, said 'thank you' to Francoise and in a moment he was gone.

6

' What da Funk,' greeted Ax from the London office.

' Extraordinary,' said Funky into the mobile handset, clamped to his ear as if he was listening to the sea in a conch. Ax related to him exactly what Maz had described to her about the drama of studio 7.
Funky listened avidly.
'Extraordinary, how amazingly extraordinary. Far out….' Lake could overhear excerpts. ' Bridges, runner eh, who'd have thought it? Bridges. And this Maz bitch. Ax, repeat to me exactly the words she's using on this show….extraordinary. She said that? Call the suits right now. You getting me?'

' Suits?' said Ax

' Yeah. We need lawyers. We are talking plagiarism. Big time.'

' Funk, I'll move on it right now.' Ax seemed reluctant. It wouldn't exactly enhance her Tuesday night Krug evenings with Maz. In the receiver of her phone she could just hear Funky and Lake talking together.
Then Ax heard Funk say to her, 'just my joke, my little jest. May be we'll go somewhere different with this. Too many suits in the world anyway.'
He flipped the mobile shut. Lake looked at Funk.
' What you looking at Lake? Seen something beautiful?'

She smiled. Funky seemed to mellow with every ray that fell on him. No gloating, crowing, strutting. Well, may be some strutting. As she said he was location specific. Or maybe it was her. Perhaps Funk was like that all along. Just needed to get an ocean between him and Bridges to replace his male rivalry with – could it be – magnanimity, generosity, security.

Lake smiled at Funk. There he was standing at the edge of the sea, trousers rolled up, handkerchief on his head, a cross between Johnny Rotten and Mahatma Gandhi. This could be the start of something really beau…extraordinary, thought Lake.
She ran her hand through her hair, that black mane flecked by white sand. But where did she really fit in to the Healing Beach? Funky's beach. The glow of the lights from a TV studio may not be as wholesome as the light from the sun but they would fall on her only. Natasha Lake, writer, broadcaster, example to a generation, Funky adjunct.
' Funk,' she said.

' Not now Lake, gotta beach to run.'

7

On the third day Guy descended into total blackness. He gazed out of the Eurostar window. He was deep in the tunnel. Staring into the glass his reflection met him. Beyond that concrete holding back an overwhelming force. The three days after the TV show were a sea of nothingness. Guy had walked out of studio 7 and just kept on walking. He walked all night. There was no time. Nothing. He must have reached his house, fell into more of a coma than a sleep. When he awoke he patted his jacket pockets. It was a reflex. He felt the outline of a wallet, passport. Guy always did travel

light, wherever he went in the world. The he began walking again. He found himself at Waterloo international terminal, where so many of his trips had started. They said to him ' you're in luck, sir.'
Guy stared back at the booking clerk. ' Luck' he mouthed silently.
In the first class carriage he fell asleep again. He woke an hour later, stared at the black reflection and fell asleep again. At Paris Gare du Nord a gloved hand fell on his shoulder.

' Monsieur, le train est terminé.'

The walking began again. Long, wide, tree lined streets, a square then a bridge. Cars on the wrong side of the road. It was dark, raining. Guy sat under the bridge. Silence except for the distant hum of traffic. A figure approached him. Holding out his hand, wanting something from him. Guy patted his pockets. He produced his wallet and looked at it without interest. The figure in front of him still had his arms outstretched, fingers protruding from sawn-off gloves. Guy placed the wallet in the man's hand. He heard a muffled word, sounded like ' mercy, mercy.' The figure disappeared and Guy was again alone in blackness.

Time passed. Hours, days, Guy wasn't measuring anything. This really was a perpetual present. No past, no future. By day he walked. His route was grew to a regular circle, the routine of the lost. Churches, parks, bringing him back to the bridge at dusk. Three times the figure appeared, in his gloves torn pieces of bread. He gave Guy a liquid to drink direct from a bottle. It burned his throat. When the light returned the walk began again. The rain stopped, weak sunshine appeared. At a crossroad he chose to go straight on. Guy stood before a church in a square. It was the first time for days he had looked around him with eyes that saw anything. Had he been there before?

8

Ax had left hours ago. By the sofa a bottle of champagne was upturned in an ice bucket, the ice now warm water. Maz wrote in her journal:

'the journey of a thousand miles begins with a single step.
I have travelled to the other side of the world and back just to start again.
I have accepted, I have learned, what have I given, what have I taught?'

9

The planning for Shore Thing was at an advanced stage. The concept was In Your State meets Celebrity Turnaround. Toby had pitched the idea to Funky only days after Guy's disappearance from screen and studio. Toby was still working in a condition of rage.
' Bridges will never be on TV again. World –wide. That man is so over.'

' You are controlling the world now?' said Funky.

' In effect. Me, Du Pont Television, your North Amercan profile. The guy is history.'

' I'm feeling that you don't like the geezer, Toby?'

Toby expressed surprise that Funky wasn't dancing on the beach at Guy's so public demise.
' You going soft or something, you sybaritic bastard. Been in the sun too long?'

' Cool it Toby,' said Funky. You could actually hear him smiling on the phone.
' I never do anything in anger. I never get involved in projects derived by angry people.'

Toby had the feeling Funky was actually going to hang up on him. Funky seemed happy to let the silence go on. Then he said. 'Why don't you come over to the Beach, Toby? First class flight on me. We need to discuss this face to face.'

The producer needed no further encouragement. Two days after the telephone conversation he and Funky were on the beach. To discuss the plans for Shore Thing the two men were seated round a table, trousers rolled up, feet in the sand. A laptop was open on the table. The scene would have been over the top in an advert.
' Are you joining us, babe?' said Funk to Lake.

' Seems like a guy thing,' she said. 'You divide the world between you.'

Funky would have been happy to include Lake in the process. Before he could pursue it, Toby looked at Lake directly and said ' Mine's a Campari.' It was supposed to be funny but came out wrong, the jet lag, the sun, the unfamiliar environment. What is the etiquette for business meetings under the fronds, sea round your ankles?
Lake glared back at him. Then turned and walked back to the Beach main office on the front. She could feel the men's eyes on her.

The idea for Shore Thing was Toby's. The Healing Beach was a huge success. Individuals and small groups flew in for stays in the chalets. The facilities, designed by Lake, were beautiful. Funky gave individual tutorials based on the method he had used on his west coast tour. Treatments were available, Ayervedic medicines, Keralan massage, Tai chi. Entertainments were provided by local musicians, groups Funky knew from the world music scene passing through en route from Europe to the US. Lake's occasional after dinner readings of poetry or extracts from literary or philosophical texts on themes such as love, the stages of life, happiness, were a much commented upon success. The Healing Beach was a fabulous formula.
Shore Thing would combine the ambience and warmth of the beach with the aggression tinged edge of Celebrity Turnaround. The technique Funky had used at the Hollywood Bowl, and imitated by Maz on the first London broadcast of the show was terrific TV. Toby loved it. He expounded the idea with enthusiasm, pausing periodically to look round for a Campari.

The format was basically the same as the London Celebrity Turnaround. Toby wanted Maz on the project. She'd done well in London and came over well on TV. But with Funky on board you had a real showman. There would be two slots. Firstly, Maz doing a one to one section then the tour de force, Funky doing a group session. Beamed direct from the beach to Toby's channel in the UK, Du Pont in Paris syndicating the show throughout Europe. Funky and Maz would each receive a fee but Funky would also receive a percentage of the syndication rights and his company would exclusively own the North American rights.

' Lot of bread there, man,' said Funky. He was thinking of himself, of Lake and his office overheads in London and the US.

' You up for it? Yes or No?' said Toby.

Lake reappeared. She carried a tray above her head in a parody of a poolside waitress. She set one glass down on the table and poured Funk a Red Stripe, leaning forward, her cleavage visible only to him. Toby looked at Funky's beer then had to swivel round to look at Lake.
' We seem to be out of Campari,' she said and sashayed off.

' Yeah, I'm up for it,' said Funky, froth on his smiling lips.

' What da Funk' said Lake as he entered the office. Toby was still on the beach, typing into the laptop.

' Nice one, Lake' replied Funky, giving her a kiss.

' I hope you know where you are going with this,' said Lake.

' To the bank. To the beach. To bed.' said Funky, putting his arm around her. She remained still, inert. The usual tossing of the mane strikingly absent noted Funky.

' It's time for me to go Funk. This is your island. Your beach, your concept.
I'm going back to London. It's been fun, but I can't be an adjunct any longer.'

Funky stared straight back at her. She was serious. It was the first time she had ever seen him taken aback. The silence went on. Lake had to steel herself not to break it or she never would go back. If she went back on her decision she would lose herself. Funky spoke first. What he said surprised her.
' I love and respect you so much I will always encourage you to do what is right for you above the desire to keep us together.'

She looked back at Funk. He still had a handkerchief on his head. She hugged him, laughing and crying.
' My beautiful pirate.'

In the morning she was gone.

10

Guy was sitting on the quayside staring into the black river. The expression " down and out" played through his mind. " Down" from where, what is there to go " up" to?
And why can't you just say " down." What does the " and out" add ? Down must be the lowest point. Beyond this you cannot fall. Out of a society, a mainstream, a reference point. What was Guy feeling? Cold, hungry? Yes at that moment, although his companion at the bridge continued to appear with the bread, and even camembert, and the bottle of burning liquid. Guy hadn't lost his memory. He hadn't forgotten who he was, his other life still only a train ride away if he could buy a ticket back into it. He

even started conversations with other riverside denizens in his Leeds Grammar School French about his travels around the world, books he had written, women he had met, being on TV. As time passed he began to wonder if he should go back. Should, ought, words in the past he had suggested people avoid. There are he remembered saying no shoulds or oughts, it isn't the way to conduct a life. He was a real Left Bank philosopher. If he had abilities, abilities to change, help, develop people shouldn't he be doing something other than simply passing time, existing? What about the need to belong, to honour your past, to contribute, to realise potential? He thought about the " and out" bit. A cop out, a return to childishness, not to be irresponsible but to have no responsibilities. He ate and slept and kept warm enough to continue. He knew of other worlds, shouldn't he be unsatisfied with this one? The river didn't examine why it flowed. But he couldn't deny he had the ability to examine how he had got here. Yet he almost seemed to like it. A release from performance, of self, of sophisticated interaction. Here if he was offered bread he took it. He could continue for another day. The snowdrops came in the parks, then the daffodils. The present without end.
Down and out. Up and in. He was just where he was. Simple.

As time flowed, Guy was increasingly self-aware. Aware he was living between two worlds, the one he had walked out on, the one he walked around in now. When he thought about it at all. The simple perpetual present was almost enjoyable. He had just enough to eat. Some evenings he was even aware of assuming an old role in drastically new surroundings. Around a brazier under the bridge various tramps gathered. Some of them nasty and dangerous. Some bizarrely ordinary. Others too had mental links back into a world they had left. Real names here didn't matter. Even in this world Guy's reputation spread. Guy was becoming known as L'Anglais qui ecout. The Man Who Listens. He heard stories of others, like himself, who had simply walked away from established lives. Some had specific reasons. Others seemed to have none. Just walked away. Some sought Guy out. Offered him food or drink to listen. A few of these later disappeared, choosing to renounce the life of the down and out riverbankers. Guy didn't analyse it. That was from the old world. His days were spent walking. Streets wide and narrow, trees with buds, parks, squares and churches. It seemed to him he could probably go on like this forever. When he thought about it at all.

Guy punctuated his circuit with stops in churches. Big, small, dark or bright. Once he felt deep within his pocket and found a single pound coin. Automatically he placed the coin in the box marked " candles 1 euro" and took out a creamy candle.
  The inscription above the candle box read:

Lighting a candle is
- a response to beauty
- thought for others
- offering of oneself.

It was exactly what Guy said to himself when he lit candles, as he had all his life, in Christ Church Cathedral, York Minster, Notre Dame…
For a moment he thought about beauty. Beautiful places, beautiful music, beautiful women. Lake, Du Pont.

He transferred the light from an already lit candle to his new one. He wondered who had lit that burning candle, hoping they were a good person. What prayer they had

said, who they had dedicated it too, the story that brought them there? The candle had been burning a long time. The flame suddenly flared up, as candles do when they are about to go out, the wick overextended, bright and smoky. As Guy's new candle took hold and in the final flare of the old candle, the gloom of the left bank church momentarily lifted. The whirl of the smoke made Guy look round. A well- dressed woman left the second row and walked away, with impeccable deportment, down the central aisle towards the exit. The draft from the door finally extinguished the candle, presumably her candle. She intrigued Guy for a moment when she was in his line of vision yet still in the sepulchral nave. One of Guy's favourite words came to his mind " silhouette" – a beautiful silhouette. A year ago, a month ago such a woman might have fascinated Guy totally. Guy had no more thoughts for her as soon as he could no longer see her. He lived in a perpetual now. In the church was one candle, one person. Guy resumed his nowness. The air became still again. Guy's undedicated, unprayed over candle grew in confidence and burned brightly. Guy simply stared at it.
Still, staring, for an age, until his candle too flared up, then died away. Guy left the darkened Church and resumed his circular walk.

The candle became Guy's watch, as accurate as any Breitling. His circular walks led him to the same church each day. Like any self-respecting tramp Guy had his own patch. The river, the left bank churches, the gardens, the churches, the river. He arrived just in time to light his candle from the adjacent candle. Guy was still sufficiently Guy Bridges to make a note of how many Euros he would owe the diocese at some future point, when he would presumably have money again, to pay for all the candles he had now taken without payment. It was symptomatic of his descent, the nadir, the remnants of the old life, the basic character. He knew he was still Guy, too honest to take candles from a church, the unformulated thought there would be a life when he had money again. Whatever your place in the journey, ascent, descent, plateau, there is always a you-ness, a Guy- ness, a reference point outside your self you can tie a life line too and decide you want to winch yourself back up. May be not the same you, the same Guy, how could that be so after all the walking, the changes, the water under the bridge? Guy couldn't steal candles from a church, he couldn't stop being Guy, he would walk back to himself and return.
Although the adjacent candle was always at the same level he did not always see the well- dressed woman. Sometimes the flare and whirl of smoke revealed her. Guy was still sufficiently Guy to be struck by the profile of a beautiful woman, that profile, that woman. He checked the time by the amount the candle had burned down. Clocks are not the only way to tell time.

Other times in the same church Guy was completely alone. The light flickered in his face. An idea from his previous life surfaced in Guy's mind. It wasn't that he wanted to go back, he wanted to go on. To go on with a mission, a rescue mission, to save his fellow tramps. The down and outs, Bridges included, would go up and onwards together like a story from the Old Testament, the re-entry of the relinquished.

Word spread quickly. Guy first told Mr Sawn –Off Gloves, who told Ms FireWater, who told Mr Meticulous Blanket Folder who…In their world you couldn't say "start at 3pm" or " Please prepare a 200 word personal statement so Mr Bridges can maximise the time available." It was simply meet by the bridge at dusk. Braziers were lit. Figures gathered, some who Guy had seen before, others from other districts, encampments, incomers. The scene was a cross between Brueghel and a Paris by night brochure; the shadowy scruffs occasionally illuminated in the floodlights of the Bateau Mouche. Huge shadows splayed across the walls of Notre Dame. A down and out's shadow is the same as a billionaires. Guy felt at home. He'd never really thought the event through, there weren't many precedents for evenings like this. Bizarre expressions flitted into Guy's minds he looked around at his cast, his audience-

"physician cure thyself"
"in the kingdom of the blind the one-eyed man is king"
"the path to power lies in acceptance, not judgement, accept everything, judge nothing."

Sitting in the churches in the candle glow Guy had felt sure this was the right thing to do. Now as the throng gathered around him their faces lit by the braziers Guy's certainty deserted him. If he was so great why was he there? Was he the divorced marriage counsellor, the bankrupt financial advisor? Why assume that the " up" world was any better than the " down and out one." Questions chattered.   Suppose they – or we if Guy included himself - had chosen this world? He was playing with fire.
He began in his best French.
' My friends, it is an honour to be among you this evening, an honour, to be among you who I have come to know as my friends, a family of souls, a society no better or worse than any other. Some people may call this an underworld,' said Guy his hand sweeping around the bank of fires, broken glass and sodden cardboard, ' but that is a judgement. In the past, my past life, like many of you I had a job, money. Now we are here not to discuss the past but the beyond now, the future. In my job I helped people. If I can give something to you, help you, that is what I want. If you want to stay here forever that is your choice. If you want to go back, go on, go up, perhaps I can help you, I make no judgement…'

' You're making a speech. A speech is a judgement'

Guy stared into the crowd. In the gloom he could make out the sharp face of a not so young young woman. Guy smiled at her and made to continue. Another voice rang out, drink-rough.

' You heard what she said, Anglais, a speech is a judgement.'

Heckle was not a word Guy had ever come across before. It flashed into his mind. Heckling. He'd made a mistake. A mistake from the other world, the world he'd left. He'd learned nothing. He should have known. Guy made another attempt to continue, to explain, to be one of the crowd. It wasn't because he wasn't working in his native language, it was because he was working in his native mind-set. He hadn't changed it enough, underneath he hadn't changed it at all.

'Who do you think you are, Anglais,' said the sharp not so young young woman. ' A preacher? Jesus?'

'Judas more like' said another, the jeer began to be taken up by several of the figures in the crowd.

It was the total opposite to what Guy had wanted. He hadn't thought about it, but his intention was good, to help, to facilitate choice, to enable people to stay or go. 'Who do you think you are, Anglais,' the woman repeated, ' what makes you think you can help us? Why do you think it is that way round?'

She was right. He opened his voice to speak, to accept, but there were no words.

Guy never thought about his exit from the society he knew. Now he never ceased to think about his apparent rejection by his adopted group, the band of riversiders, the brothers and sisters with their fiery drinks and bin-matured bread. He disappeared too from even this society, outcast from the outcast, the failure complete. The descent of the descended. The walking, the circles began again.

11

The coughing always cleared as soon as Lake stood up.
'The title of my talk today: Pyscho-Beauty. How do we know what is beautiful? Is it an external or internal concept? Do we change when we are with beautiful people and / or in beautiful places? If we are with beautiful people are we ergo in a beautiful place? Can anyone or anything become beautiful?'
As she began her oration, the two dinner guests sitting on each side of her leant forward and conversed across her.

' A talk with practical illustrations, no doubt' said one.

Lake, so accomplished now as a speaker, continued and looked around her calmly.

It was sometimes difficult to believe Oxford was a 21st century co-ed world class university. Most of the people at the high table, and all the people in the portraits hanging from the walls were men although, to be fair, Lake had noticed even in the last few years the ratio of men to women in the floor was now more 50-50. As she rose to speak she always tried to shut these thoughts out. They weren't helpful. She was speaking. It was now. She wasn't a sociologist. She wasn't averse to being thought beautiful. She only objected to people, men and women thinking that was it. The packing was the content, the exterior was the interior. Just because they couldn't think past or around it didn't mean that was what Lake deliberately wanted. Lake wanted the same as anybody else. To be taken seriously, to be listened to, for things to be just right. Ideas, fun, status. She'd had heads of department, men and women, leaving their arms of welcome around her lower back two seconds too long. Her back stroked- yes - and her ideas pinched. That was in the past. Fun is fun, but being messed around by people who pretended they were above everything was so infuriating. There was that debate a few years back when a philosophy don said in a claret infused drawl that her ideas had as much depth as the front of her jacket. Lake then played the game. There was always that dread of being regarded as unfunny, a spoilsport. " I'm glad you think I'm such a deep thinker." There was an uneasy laugh around the hall, but Lake decided that was the last time it would ever happen. What she decided happened.

Her oration drew elegantly to a close:
' beauty - do you want to analyse it, experience it or be it? Think about it.'

En route from Oxford to Paddington Lake philosophised on the point that no-one had ever raised so much as an eyelash, at least publicly, that time, it seemed so long ago now, when she left studio 7 with Funky. She gazed out of the window into the non-country, the endless industrial sheds, the only rural areas being the middle of roundabouts. Her face was mirrored in the window. Still beautiful, reflective.

' Bastards all,' said Ax to the assembled company as Lake related the story of the Don, the Claret and the jacket. Ax had invited Lake along to one of her evenings chez Maz. Champagne flowed, opinions were exchanged, stories aired. Lake related more inside stories of the patronising, hypocrites she had agreed to put up with at Oxford. The frightened men and anxious women of the high tables. Ax related sagas of her and Funk in the early days on the road. Maz, the guilt of plagiarism mixing with the bubbles of champagne stared into a middle distance. Ax and Lake were riffing across the sullen Maz, dividing the quota of her silence between them. Lake told the story of Funk and Toby on the beach vividly. It was a great image.
Funk was Funk. Toby was a jerk. A rude, crass, on the make, powerful jerk.

' How has Funk changed on the island?' asked Ax to Lake.

' You know him better than I do really,' replied Lake.

' I never went to bed with him.'

' Excuses, regrets, inadmissible,' said Maz.

' He seems a bit mellower, more generous, more patient. Can't place it exactly. He's easier to deal with now.' said Ax.
' Sex on the beach. Changes everybody, it's so beautiful.' said Lake. Maz looked at her eyes turned slightly upwards, middle distance focus, back on the beach.

' Wouldn't know,' said Maz.

' Self pity. Inadmissible,' said Ax.
Lake told them more of her adventures with Funky on the island. Maz told them how she felt when she found out Bridges had pulled the plug on her expenses. Ax listened for as long as she was able before cutting in.
' They are just men. Who needs 'em.'

She opened another bottle of Krug. Ax knew how to open champagne without the pop and spurt. Lake and Maz listened as she related her adventures in California with Martine. It was well past midnight when Lake stood up, tossed back the trade mark sheeny mane, and held up her glass toast-like.
' Men, who needs ' em,' she heard herself say.

' Cliché, doesn't become you,' said Maz to Lake without looking at her. ' It's been a lovely evening. I feel glad to be part of this. But I'm different to you.'

'How so, Mazzo' said Ax. ' You all do pair work. I mean worky work as well as the love-sex routine. Ax – Funk, Ax – Martine. Lake – Funky, Funky – Lake.'

'Bridges – Jasminder Khalm?' said Lake and Ax together.

' No' , said Maz, her hand caressing her own cheek, ' we were just in the same room together.'

It was early afternoon when Ax entered the Richmond office next day. Same time as Funky used to bounce in. She checked the faxes and emails from The Beach. There was a fax from Toby's TV company. Copied to Martine who was now running the office on The Beach in Lake's absence and to Du Pont Broadcasting in Paris.
Subject: Shore Thing.
Toby outlined the finalised format for the show. It was now essentially a Funky showcase. Maz would introduce the show from The Beach, support the turnarounds and summarise, top and tail as Toby put it. Funk would take a gaggle of celebs together and work with them in his signature tough love style. Test Match Special style commentary on the proceedings would be provided by a panel chaired by Maz, consisting of Lake and an as yet unspecified other.
' What a bleedin' circus,' thought Ax.

12

Churches had always been sanctuaries for Guy. He didn't go to Church, he went to churches. And Guy was still Guy. Not religious but spiritual. As a young man in Leeds, Oxford or London he would sometimes leave a shop or pub or library and simply sit in a church. Any church, didn't have to be a Wren or Hawksmoor. Sometimes he'd light a candle, make up prayers of his own. Nothing to do with Jesus. Silent chants, peace, recognition of himself, the abundance in his life. Just as a Christian could say a prayer in a pub or shop or library he could contemplate or take time out in a church. The churches on his daily route now were always dark, only candlelit. He felt most pleased when a choir or organist was rehearsing. It was like a bonus. By now he was beginning to look most un-Guy like. The well-kept hair a mat, the shiny shoes now split, the beard. No one ever bothered him. His eyes stared with rejection. He rarely looked about him.
In a mirror above the font of one Left Bank church Guy stopped for long enough to study his reflection.
It had been so long since Guy had either a mirror or a reflecting person to see himself in, what he had become. The face shocked the essential him. The image in the reflection jolted against the image of himself he still maintained in his mind. Guy knew he could close this gap between the image he saw in the mirror and the essential image he held of himself. He could rise again, be illuminated by reflection, by light, by decision.

Guy realised again he felt drawn to this church, his walks had led him here not exactly by design, not exactly by accident or randomness. This one on the left bank, he felt he had been to before. When? How? The spring sunshine activated his memory, thawed the nowness. In the gladed church yard glossy media types came to eat their lunch. One of these types, a woman seemed to exude a kind of fragile power. When Guy passed she looked at him. Her hand made an involuntary movement across her chest. In fear of a vagrant or in a glimmer of recognition? Less than a second later she raised her bottle of Badoit water. That was it, the label on the bottle of water. Guy had naturally orientated himself to this area because his Paris seminars were always in this area. He always took his Badoit water and fresh air break in this church. He wasn't the old Guy but retained the same Guy – youness.

Then Guy now remembered how healthy he was in those days, Badoit rather than fire – water, well – prepared, regular food, not only food, meals. He wanted to be healthy again. Be wholly aware of himself.

The Church was off a busy office strewn street – fashion boutiques, media houses abounded - in a leafy square, an oasis. One showery day that Spring he saw her inside the church - second row. The shiny buttons in her boxy suit, the sliver of silver, confirmed the memory. He hadn't really spoken to a woman for ages. Guy missed that too now. But the renascent Guy wanted to speak to rejoin contact rather than speak to impress. He sat next to her. She froze, shocked, perhaps afraid.
' Why do you always sit in the second row?' he said in English.
She looked up, stared at him, then lowered her head again. People like her don't know people who look like him.

' Everywhere I went you were always sitting in the second row. Not the front, not the back, the second. Must be a reason.'

She stared at him again.
' Guy Bridges. No. Is it? Guy Bridges? The Guy Bridges. What are you doing here? What happened ? You need help.'

' And you, Francoise du Pont, what do you need? Do you believe you will find it here?' She continued to stare at him. Eventually she said, 'maybe I will, maybe I will.'

Then she stood up. From bowed supplicant to decisive business tycoon in one movement. She put her manicured hand on his frayed suit.

' You know that was the only thing I never liked about your act, the way you dressed. The best tailor in Paris is a street away from here. We are going back up.'

' I'm the only one who is down and out.'

' You're the only one who looks it.'

13

From her apartment Guy could see over the whole city. He looked back at the bridge in the distance. Francoise Du Pont was on the phone the whole time, switching between French and English. A hairdresser appeared. Guy was pushed back into an expensive armchair and a shroud wrapped round his neck. The Parisian barber's scissors flashed working through the neglect like a topiarist redefining a garden. As the old new Guy emerged Du Pont spoke excitedly.
' I've done it. I've got you back on.'

' On what?'

' On TV. Toby said you'd never go on TV again. Worldwide. It isn't too wise for him to disagree with me.'
' Supposing I don't want to go back on.'

' You have to.'

' I don't have to do anything,' said Guy, rising from the chair, only one half of his hair cut.

Du Pont and the hairdresser pushed him back.
' You helped me. London, Rotterdam, the East coast US. I was always there. You turned me round as some might put it. I can help you. Organisationally.'

' I don't need help.'

' You do Guy, everyone does. We all need help, we all need to learn, we all…'

' I have every thing I need.'

They pushed Guy back again.
' You are being selfish. You are not listening.'

' Me, selfish? Look at me.'

' Exactly. Self indulgence. Running away. Withdrawing your gifts. That's selfish. If it was just you Guy I'd leave you to it. But it isn't only you, it is the path you embody. Like it or not Guy you are a giver. That's what you are here to do.'

' No. And the idea of calling me selfish is risible.'

' It is not risible at all. You have helped a lot of people. Including me. And including yourself. Who are you Guy Bridges? Who will you be ? You cannot choose to be a tramp. You haven't earned it. You cannot choose not to be Guy Bridges. It wouldn't be wise. It wouldn't be fair and it isn't right.'

' Fair? Right?'

' You have helped people, but it isn't altruism. You may claim the money is incidental. The other guy –Funky- is the materialist. I'm not so sure. But you have done things the right way. You chose the right way to help people. If you don't go on the wrong way to help people will prevail. You have to go on Shore Thing or your whole path will be false. If your path is false so is mine and everyone else who you have ever helped.'

Guy stared back at her. She touched his face where the barber had nicked his skin shaving off the beard. She was right. Guy Bridges was bigger than himself.

14

From the diary of Francoise Dupont:

' It isn't everyday someone rescues somebody.'

VI

1

When the student is ready the teacher appears. Francoise was teaching Guy his own path. It was now only days before the first broadcast of Shore Thing. Guy became Guy again remarkably quickly. In the planning meetings in London before they were due to fly out to The Beach Guy had shown a new assertiveness in negotiating a deal with Toby. Francoise wondered if he was trying to impress her. In pulling Guy literally out of the gutter Francoise had shown great wisdom, patience and insight. She was using Guy's own skills to allow him to ease his own way back. He paid her the compliment of using the business skills he had learned to negotiate the right fee and format from Toby. The producer foresaw only one problem. Why should Funky allow Guy on his beach?

' What the Funk?' Toby spoke aloud as the final teleconference commenced.

It was so clear you could actually hear the crash of Atlantic waves in the background.

' Where's Lake?' was all Funky said.

' Lake is on board,' said Toby.

' I asked you where she is, not where she's at.'

' Somewhere between Oxford and London Paddington, last we heard. Shall we get on to business?'

' I've gone far enough on this one, man.' Funky came back. 'I'm even working with Bridges. Get Lake online now or I'm back on the beach without any of you losers.'

Before Toby could retort anything terminal like " be reasonable Funk" the door opened. All the faces swung round to fix on Lake.

' Do you wait behind doors to make entrances like that?' said Francoise, recognising a fellow class act. It would be rude not to stare at Lake.

' I'm here babe,' she said into the speaker phone.

' Lake. Beautiful coincidence.' It was strange hearing Funky's voice floating round the room, feeling his presence, seeing nothing.

' Design not coincidence, Funk, that's were it's at.' Lake's voice had a new edge. It suited her, suited this context.

' Mind if we talk business, love birds?' Francoise wanted closure. Now Lake was in Funky was less likely to reject Bridges.

Toby chaired the teleconference. It was a new form of technology for him, unclear whether the physical advantage was being present in London or invisible yet audible from The Beach. ' I'll open the proceedings' he began. ' Present here in London: me, Guy Bridges – looking remarkably well if I may say so old fruit all things considered - Francoise Du Pont, Lake. Apologies received from Miss Khalm. She rang me yesterday. In the USA Martine, Louisa - May. With Funky on The Beach, Alexandra. Stars all.'

'You cool with this. You cool with me, Lake?' Funk checked in again.

' Let's rock, Funk,' said Toby into the speakers. ' money is time.'

Deals made, arrangements finalised, money talked. Shore Thing had all the logistics of a latter day Rolling Stones tour. Towards the end of the conference suits appeared wheeled in by Toby and Francoise to lock up the deal. Maz out. Lake in. Three shows featuring one slot each from Funky and Bridges. Lawyers and accountants always brought out the old hippy in Funky, even though he had now long been a millionaire. Guy could present himself as before, the straight ahead professional, with Francoise covering the business for him, for them, trustworthy and elegant, knowing precisely what she was good at.

' It's a wrap,' said Toby. Guy and Francoise smiled at each other. Funky and Lake, in their own spaces, looked straight ahead into the now disconnected speaker phones. Perhaps if you held the receiver to your ear you could hear the sound of the ocean.

2

' Been a while,' drawled Funky.
Guy shielded his eyes as Funky eclipsed out of the full island sun in his white suit. On one arm Lake. The other arm outstretched. For a less than a second they faced each other like an Israeli PM meeting a PLO leader. Then Guy too reached out and took Funky's hand with pleasure. That firm assertive no-need-to-prove-anything original Bridges handshake seemed to have survived his days as a down and out. Guy kissed Lake – on both cheeks, more chivalrous than lascivious.
' Better than studio 7,' smiled Guy.

' Studio 7 is the past,' said Funky.
There was a silence.

' I'd like you to like me,' said Guy.' I always liked you, in so far as I knew you.'

' I never liked you,' replied Funky pleasantly. ' But then I never much liked myself. Like is a funny word. Soft, meaningless, unnecessary. People confuse like with validation. I validate myself. I don't do like. I do love. Love of my life is Lake.'

' Like the speech, Funk' laughed Lake. 'Love of your life is Funk.'

The carefree toss of the mane was back. The silence fell again, an easy silence of equals, the lapping sound of the waves ameliorating the tapping of the TV crews building the set.

3

Shore Thing was the most successful show on TV. Ever. Worldwide. After the first two shows Toby and the suits, sated by ratings, left them to it. By popular consent honours were even between Guy and Funky. They had both " turned round" some heavy duty people before your very eyes. Francoise was so proud of Guy. " My Guy" she called him when they were alone together. They never talked of how she allowed him to winch himself up from those city gutters. Guy's success on the shows validated how he had helped her in the past, how he had contributed to the essence of her identity.

From the wings Francoise looked on as the music faded out at the top of the third show. The immaculate Lake strode on, her stillness entrancing.
' Welcome to you, wherever you are in the world, whoever you are, however you are,' said Lake. 'It's our third edition of Shore Thing, the last in the current series.' There were groans of despair from the audience banked up around a hemisphere stage erected on the beach. ' Yes, I know how much people all around the world love seeing and learning from the amazing changes we see enacted before us on the show. The last in the current series, but I feel sure we'll be back.' Cheers from the audience.
' You never know what the future will bring.' She said, off script. ' Now, let's hear it, here is Guy Bridges.'

Applause rippled out. Not cheers or whistles or air klaxons but strong, meaningful applause. Guy, smart, relaxed, Guy-like, was bathed in light centre stage.
' What's happening today Guy on Shore Thing?'

' Thanks Natasha. As you said today is the last in the current series so something different. So far this show has been about celebs. But what is a celeb but a reflection of ourselves? Everyone is a celeb, no one is a celeb. I'm going to ask someone from our audience, anyone, with any issue to come forward. Come forward, share with us your issue, not a problem but a challenge in your life. Some point that other people can relate to. You know that feeling when you are at a meeting and you want to ask a question but daren't because you think it is too obvious. Then some other brave soul asks the question you all wanted to ask. Come forward. We are all the same, all living a life together, making sense of signs, gifts…'

Maz appeared form the crowd, walked forward and stood in front of Guy and Lake. Lake did the usual introductions.
' You are live on Shore Thing. You are among friends. We welcome you. Everything you say is confidential, it's just you, me, Guy and everyone in the world.'
Lake and Guy never missed a beat. No one even knew Maz was on the island. She really was a face from the crowd. They were professionals and life is live. Shore Thing was true to life. No rehearsals.

' My name is Jasminder Khalm. People call me Maz.'

' Welcome Maz. Where are you from?' asked Lake in MC mode.

' Does it matter?'

' No. But people like to place people. Of course if you are hiding someth…'

' Thanks, Natasha. I'll take this from here on in. You've done the introductions. We have all we need to go forward.'

' You're the man, Guy,' said Lake and glided off the stage. Guy and Maz sat facing each other. As the sun set the spotlights picked them up in higher definition. Behind them the sea glimmered. As was part of the Shore Thing set a semi-circle of the helpers formed round the central couple, kneeling on one knee like figures in a nativity play.

' Jasminder, welcome. We don't need to know where you are from but why you are here, why you came forward to share your experience with us.'

' Thank you Guy,' said Maz looking directly at him, composed but burdened.

' What do you think we can learn from you?' started Guy.

' You? Learn from me? I don't think anyone can learn anything from me. That is why I came forward. I am a shell, a husk, I take, I am nothing, I have no identity.'
The spotlights intensified. The audience was focussed. After all, this person had emerged from them. How would Bridges deal with this? Where would he go with it?

' So you say no one can learn anything from you but you have learned to say you are a shell, a husk with no identity.'

There was a silence from Maz. The close ups on the screens revealed tears in her eyes though she was not actually crying. There was a hardness around her. The audience were still through intrigue not sympathy.
Guy continued, step by step, working through challenge, the person confronting themselves.
' So you have learned at least one thing: you haven't learned. Tell me something else you have learned.'

' You will receive more by giving than taking. Learn what you can but make it your own. Acknowledge others.'

' You said you hadn't learned anything, you seem to know a lot. Why did you think you were a shell?'

' Did?'

' You learned in the past, you are learning now. You just said yourself. " You will receive more by giving than by taking." You are giving to all these people, you are being true to yourself, so you are not a shell.'

Guy gestured to all the people around them. The darkness grew, you couldn't see individuals in the audience, simply a single mass.
Maz looked at Guy. Tears were streaming down her face in complete silence.

' Be true to yourself Jasminder. Learn and give. You will have helped more people than you realise. Not all ideas are original. Development is original, confronting your emptiness and learning to keep learning is your role. Then you can give back.'

Guy looked out to the audience.
' Who here has never been helped, never received anything, however big or small?'
No one moved.
' I have been helped too,' continued Guy,' by friends, by strangers, people I thought I was in competition with, people who I thought could give me nothing, only take. Even the wisest person takes, even the simplest person can give.'

Guy thought of room 208, of the tramps by the river, of Francoise. It was live TV. Guy knew the demands of the medium, the deal. Guy and Maz never acknowledged there and then they had met before. It was a different life. The audience needed a punch line, a transformation.
' You emerged from this crowd Jasminder. Be accepted back into it, them, your friends, well-wishers. The authentic you. It isn't what you have learned, picked up. It's what you have put down – yourself. You're not built on anything, so you copied more than you learned. Now go back to the start. Take the time. Add what you have learned from others to what you know about yourself. Then you will be you. You will be a learning, giving you.'
Guy played the crowd. 'What don't we like?'

' Takers,' they chanted back.

' Who do we love?'

' Givers, learners, listeners.'

' Go back to the start Jasminder. Take the time and we will love the learning giving you.'

The spotlight followed Maz as she walked proudly back into the crowd.
Applause rippled round the auditorium for Guy, growing louder.
The spotlight went up again on Lake.
' Let's hear it for Mr Guy Bridges,' said Lake, working the crowd. 'And now…'
The audience knew the structure, what was coming next. Lake's link was lost in a growing chorus of ' What da Funk, WHAT DA FUNK.' Cheers, whistles, air klaxons rang out over the beach.
The spotlight picked out Funky centre stage. He raised his arms signalling the crowd to cut the applause. He wasn't so vain to need it but wouldn't feel aggrieved if it continued. After all it was already triple the length and volume Bridges had received. Finally you could hear Funky's voice.
' Nice one Lake, beautiful. And Bridges too. No one like him. He's the real deal, class act. A hard act to follow but…'

' WHAT DA FUNK' roared back the crowd on cue.

' You are too kind,' responded Funky, loving it, relaxed, smiling, at home.

' Bridges is right. Enough of the celebs. Tonight is your night,' he continued his arm sweeping the crowd. Searchlights scanned the mass, fleetingly targeting individuals.

' It is our last night. We're gonna go out in a blaze of positive energy, there is nothing we cannot do together, we just have to believe. Isn't that right Lake?'
Lake had stayed on stage. Not the usual format when Guy or Funky were working their magic. Funky was pleased. She was his crowd of one. Funky turned it on.
' You all know we are not here to play games or even to have fun…'

' Tell 'em like it is Funk,' shouted some voices gospel style , safe in the blackness.

' …this is like it is. We are not here to play games. The game is over. Games we all play. All of us, me, Lake, Bridges, every single one of you will leave here today as different people. You are all liars and frauds, you all live behind a front, on a foundation of excuses. Is there any one here who will challenge my assumption?'

The amazing silence commenced. Thousands of people. Every press article written about Funky's sessions had to include the expression you could hear a pin drop. There was no way round it. The contrast between the welcome he received when he walked on the stage – the cheers, whistles, klaxons – and this moment was always deeply impressive. The silence was the cure. The silence continued and continued. A single spotlight on Funky as he stared back at the audience. He was just about to recommence when it happened.

' I do,' said Lake.

' Lake?'

' I do. I challenge your assumption. I am not a liar or a fraud. I do not live a life of excuses.'

The audience released a collective gasp. There were now two spotlights on the stage, one on Funky, the other on Lake. They were held together by a beam of light.
Individual voices began to break out of the crowd. Maybe she's right, they murmured audibly. The spell was broken. Funky didn't try to rescue it. Another voice suddenly rang out round the auditorium. It was Bridges.
' She is right Funky. We do not all live a life of lies and excuses. Not all of us. Not all the time.'

' Lake. And you Bridges?'

Guy, Natasha Lake and Funky were centre stage each in their own pool of light.
 Bridges continued.
' Your model is based on aggression. Sometimes it works, sometimes it doesn't. It makes a spectacular show. But we are individuals not a crowd. We have to embrace each other not confront. Listen. Learn. Start over and over again. You aren't giving any more, Funk. You've gone as far as this will take you. You had something to say then you became a showman. A gauntlet thrower.'
Funky stared back at Bridges. Then turned to Lake, his eyes full of questions.
Lake simply mouthed back to him ' he's right.' Then she said out loud with a smile:

' Time to move on Funk. On from The Beach. New us, new model. You, we and start again, on our beach.'

Silence descended again. Then Guy walked over to Funky and embraced him. On the big screens you could see Funky melt, arms at first stiff with surprise before he returned the embrace as warmly as it was given.
Lake said into the microphone, 'competition is over, we can all learn from each other.'
Audience participation grew. Shouts rang out:
' Show is over Funk.'

' No aggression, no confrontation.'

' Listen to Bridges.'

' Give Lake a kiss, man.'
Bridges stepped back into the shadows, as Lake kissed Funky centre stage.
The kiss seemed to go on forever. The audience began to cheer and wolf whistle.
The spotlight fell finally on Lake only.
' You are all givers, winners,' she said. ' The same tides wash every beach. But I think we need our beach back right now.'

VII

Next day Funky and Natasha lay in the dunes the stage set had imprinted in the sand.

Natasha Lake wrote in her journal:
'a cataclysm is an evolution that happens to you in an instant.'
Source: unknown

' That is so beautiful,' said Funk.

In North London Maz put her old journal in the recycling bin, then her pen hovered over the blank page one of a new note book, picture of Sydney Harbour Bridge on the cover.

By the Pacific Ax and Martine checked the trans Atlantic best seller lists and smiled at the triple joint firsts in the non fiction sections.

In Paris Francoise wrote in her journal a quote:

' Each friend represents a world in us. A world possibly not born until they arrive and it is only by this meeting that a new world is born.'
Source: Anais Nin

She thought of showing it to Guy but he seemed at one with own thoughts as he gazed out of her window across the city to the bridge by river. Guy felt Francoise looking at him. In one movement he turned and smiled and embraced her. The silence was peaceful.

From the draft of the new Guy Bridges book Rivers and Islands:

' You can be whoever you want to be. Tell people who you are and that's it. If you believe it, so will they. I'm confident, I'm open, we're alright. Stand up straight, say it, you are it. You can change everything. Anything you want. Your name, the way you speak, what you say, how you listen. The colour of your shirt – lose the stripes or ditch the beige. Who cares where you are from? Do you? It's all such a long time ago. And it's getting longer by the second. Can you really reinvent yourself? Is life a circle or a straight line?'

Guy's gaze turned into a look, steadfast, out of the window, through the reflection of the inner pane. He looked, listened, felt. Felt for the lips of Francoise du Pont.
' Amazing' she said.

' You are' said Guy, his lips still on hers even as she continued to speak.

' I mean you can take a train from Paris to Leeds with just one change'

Guy smiled at her joke which only just worked, that still unplaceable accent. Arrival.

" Leeds, Leeds," blared the loudspeaker, " all change, this service terminates here."

' I'll show you some old places,' said Guy reaching for the luggage. They only had one bag between them. They left the station and walked straight across the cross roads.

' Show me the new ones too,' she said ' they must be all around us.'

WISE GUY

4 x 4

I always thought that it was a cliché. Those stories I read of Spitfire or Lancaster pilots looking down at a limb and realising they were hit and covered in blood. I mean you'd know that, wouldn't you, feel it. How could you not? Yet it took me a second, maybe more, to realise why I was on the ground, why a small area of tarmac seemed a mix of scarlet and black. I looked back. The 4 x 4 tangled with my bike now a hybrid 4 x 6. The apples from the basket, free of cellophane, had arced into the air and splattered onto the windscreen. There was a bleep and thunk. I was still on the ground figuring it all out. Footsteps. Heavy, urgent. I looked in front of me. Black boots, Birkin bag swinging. I wondered if I died and gone to another place, populated by Diana Rigg in a previous episode.

This feeling dissipated when she spoke.

' Your bloody bike has scratched my fender.'

My eyes moved further up, the old reflexes even in this situation, taking in thigh and bust before finally reaching her face ages later.

' Your bloody bike has scratched my fender,'

her voice metronomic, something sort of familiar about her.

I got to my feet to neutralise the advantage. See how I was.

'I'm fine thanks,' I said. ' No need to worry about me.'

' Your bloody bike has scratched my fender.'

I was beginning to find her repertoire rather limited.

I began to take it all in. It was like I was someone else. Her vehicle had 'sod you' written all over it. My bike a write off. Only bought it a few weeks ago. Thoughts in my head, random, useless . Why I rode a mountain bike and she drove a Cherokee Cross Country Warrior. Suppose the warrior bit may have some relevance. Her hand on hip, the bandelero style belt, the boots, the stripey upturned collar protecting her neck, top 3 buttons undone revealing a necklace with an insignia.

' Your bloody b...'

Sod this.

' What's your phone number?' I said. Even at full height she was a t least on my level, maybe even a couple of centimetres above me. Hate it when people are taller than me, especially ones who apparently have no right to ask you to look up to them.

Never been in a collision before. I had this impression of knights of the road, conversant with the high way code, PC in white traffic gloves, organising the exchange of telephone numbers, insurance companies sort it out at dawn.

' Your phone number?'

'Phone number! Bleedin' cyclist, dream on, loser.'

2 heels on tarmac, beep, thunk, swish, 4 tyres on tarmac. Not good. The remains of the bike were thrown out by the rear wheels. The car screached forward like a Harrier off a carrier. Another feel of liquid on my arm, the apple from the windscreen topping the blood on the road.

'Can you tighten up on that one even more ?' I asked the operative.

Normally I let these things go. Rise above it, don't sweat the small stuff and it's all small stuff. But blood is blood and people like that don't call people like me loser. And I thought it would look good. Actually I *was* about to let it go. The fuzz didn't really want to know, I didn't really want to bring the plod in but on the way out of the station I saw a Special coming in, exchanging his day bike helmet, for his night fuzz cap. A brother. Kind of.

' You've got the time and place,' he said ' get the congestion charge lot to get off their ass. All they do is look at CCTV all day, human face might interest them. Then again might not.'

Kind of felt he knew whose side he was on despite the LAPD style pronunciation, arse always seemed more honest.

The room was windowless, the CCTV footage grainy, the operative less engaging than his machine, the pin through his lip disconcerting. The frame, tightened up, was now at full magnification. The woman's neck craned forward through a smeared windscreen, the operative froze on the insignia that had swung out from the hinted cleavage. He looked at me for the first time

' Oh yeah, got your game mate,' he said,

still looking at me. I preferred it when he was in eye contact avoidance mode. For one repellent moment I thought he was actually going to wink.

I was staring at the frame, the three undone buttons, the fourth obviously under considerable pressure.

' The insignia, look…'

' Yeah, nice,' he said.

What the hell. Just walk away I said to myself.

I took a picture of the frame on my RAZR V3i.

' You're in a bad way, man' the operative said

You think *I'm* in a bad way I said to myself. Then walked away.

Had to go on foot to the meeting that night. I'd hated this assignment from the off. It's so not me. I remonstrated with the head of C section. The fact the real you hates them only means you'll do a better job for us, she said. Right of course, danger with these ops for any head of section is you just go native. Difficult not to. Eventually. When I first went in the meetings were such a shambles they made Pete Docherty look like CEO of Kinsey's.

No chair, no agenda, the leaflets always ran, the old insignia smudged. At least I think it was smudged. I could never really tell if it was a whale or tree. I hate amateurs. The longer the assignment went on the more professional they became. Even managed unanimous agreement a new insignia would be developed by brand consultancy. The bruised apples they used to bring in for the breaks gave way to a scheduled adjournment on the agenda when they had a strict 20 minute latte break at the adjacent Starbucks. I remember when I filed that in the report C said making ironic observations was always, in her experience, the first step in that ever so imperceptible process of becoming a native. She had seen it in them all. In C's view it was at precisely the time when these sort of groups put the suits on and went out to ad agencies they became so dangerous. Then in walks three buttons, the boots, the insignia almost undercover in the valley of the hilltops. She opened her Birkin to put away the pristine luminous bike clips. Naturally I made a mental note of the contents: mobile RAZR V 3i same issue as mine, Cherokee key fob.

I looked at her, she looked right back. A stare-out even a CCTV would lose.

I watched the chair come forward to meet her. Hand outstretched. Crisp, Clinton style –

you take their hand and put your other hand over the top of theirs. I remember my first meeting, hand shake limper than their allotment lettuces.

'So glad to have you with us, perhaps you'd just prefer to be an observer at your first meeting, see how it goes.'

The chair continued with a few words of welcome, dimmer switch down, beamer on, top of the agenda, *colleagues*, floor to approve the new insignia and logo the executive committee commissioned.

Dimmer up, show of hands, looked like I was the only one who didn't like it.

4x4

Armchair counsellor

In my beginning is my end.

Every love I've ever had my first and last,

There'll never be another you.

Wasn't anyone before you, never will, can't be anyone after;

Wouldn't make sense.

And things really need to make sense-

Love actually does.

Make the world go round. Really.

In my end is my beginning.

It was when we went to the counsellor to make it last

I knew it wouldn't.

She showed us into the room –

You walked right into it.

Sofa in the middle of the room,

Looked pretty well upholstered to me.

Two armchairs each side.

Your're the the lady – I let you go first.

I'm a man, I let you go first.

You sat on the armchair.

So I let you go first.

Before and after now

" Bridlington, all change, train terminates, train terminates here, All change!"

Change, terminate, terminate, change. What can it mean? To my astonishment big sis with the single mindedness that had become so characteristic of her so quickly, suddenly pulled a leather strap, reached out, twisted something outside and the door opened. Opened onto England. My feet touched the ground. The ground held me up, same as it did in Vienna. Maybe it wasn't that different. I'd been asleep since – how do you pronounce that station – Harwich? The last thing Mama said to me was just do as your sister tells you. Do as she tells you, she is *me* now, then she disappeared in a puff of smoke. Mama said she'd be along later. Don't know why Pater wasn't at the station. Sometimes you feel you don't want answers to your questions so don't ask them. Of course I knew something was up, wasn't a holiday, I mean why would we have a single ticket, wasn't even a proper ticket, more like some kind of pass book. I should know; I used to love to stand next to Pater when he bought the return tickets for Neusiedl am See.

Such authority! Two returns to Neusiedl am See he used to say, non –smoker. I always had the window seat. Collected all the numbers on the way out and on the way back. Tank engine, then the 2 – 4 – 2 express inward from Budapest. Always remember that, Pater checking his watch by it. Gosh, I've just thought first time I've been on a boat and train without Mama or Pater, maybe I'm too old now to be collecting numbers. Wish he was here though, this train you have to be outside to open the door so you can get outside.

And this unlocatable feeling we're going in the wrong direction. ' Course it was big sis who bought the tickets, not the Pater, *the*...

" Ah, yes so you must be Alfons."

The gentleman leaned forward.

" My name is…"

Suddenly the train let off a big one, huge hiss and stream of steam. I gather the English gentleman was saying his name but I couldn't catch it. I looked a t him. He was still shaking my hand. A man's handshake. He smiled. A smiling face, yes, I realise now, looking back, it was what I needed to see, a smiling face, an unthreatened face. He was still speaking. I listened to the accent, it was how we heard English in school. An English gentleman. I took my eyes away from his as he released my hand and stepped back to speak to big sis. I looked at him all over.

" Don't you know it's rude to stare, if you stare I'll leave you there.

Don't you know it's rude to stare, if you stare I'll leave you there."

Pater always used to say this on the platform at Neusiedl am See when I was mesmerised by the ladies alighting from Vienna Central back from café and cakes and whatever else they did in Stefanplatz. Of course he was secretly pleased his boy was beginning to look at *ladies*, and not only their hats. But this English gentleman… – I say gentleman because he was English so he must be, that's what we were taught by Frauelein Holz at school in our English conversation class. There was this rumour at our school of how Fraulein Holz had been trained in this college called St Hilda, but she had come back early and if anyone ever mentioned it she changed the subject…

So I took advantage of the English gentleman's engagement with big sis to stare, sort of. He was dressed all in black except for this white circular collar. Sis turned to me and said we should call him Reverend. So I did, though it seemed a funny name to me. I always thought English gentlemen would be called George or Algy or …

" Now young Alfons, you sit up here with me, you can be the navigator."
It was an Austin. Pater had a Daimler. The Rev, as sis and I came to call him, suddenly pulled out of the Bridlington station forecourt. I yelled out involuntarily and put my fingers in front of my face.
" Halt, bitte Halt!"
Sis and the Rev looked at me. Sis annoyed because we had agreed on the train we would try to speak English at all times, make Fraulein Holzelmacher proud of us, not lapse into German if we could possibly help it. The Rev because he couldn't see there was anything to shout about. I kept my hands in front of my face but opened my fingers like a fleshy blind. Of course, England. The Austin on the left, all the other Rovers, and Morris Oxfords and Triumphs and Nortons and Healeys and the names I heard about as a younger boy whizzing by on the right. I took my hands away from my face and looked. Looked around me. The red post boxes, the paned telephone boxes, the garden hedges, the bay window of the, what was that funny name, semi – detached with sticky tape over the glass, like they were expecting something to happen. Something, I could feel it, something bad, but I don't know what. At a cross roads a bobby in helmet and white gloves waved us through and - I'm sure I'm not making this up, – saluted the Rev. Sis and I looked at each other and smiled for the first time in how many days, 2 , 3 ?

I realised I
didn't know how many days since Mama had told big sis at the Zentral Station barrier to look after me on my holiday. I mean, big sis. Look after me! The other way round maybe. The longest train journey we had ever been on, the frontiers we crossed, France, Belgium, the big ship, another train, children, children everywhere and hardly any adults. What an exciting prospect it seemed. But then why hadn't Mama come too, where was Pater, why did no-one else get on or off the train, why the funny food in card board boxes, why the train that went on and on, didn't stop at the sea so we could go on the beach but just a big crocodile onto a big boat? Not even a pleasure cruiser like the ones Pater and I went on in Neusiedl. An oily dark crowded boat, children either sleeping or crying, I mean if this was a holiday God help us. Or maybe it's what the English did I thought, long train journeys, rain drops spreading horizontally mixed with streaks of soot on the window, soot that got onto my sisters best coat when she reached out of the window to open the door. Then I remembered what Pater had said to me, when I last saw him, funny armband on his suit:

" I'm going on a train too soon Alfons, perhaps further than Neusiedl, I'll come back for you, I'll never forget you."

He had this kind of smile, a smile which I'd never seen before, which gave me the creeps, a forced smile, an unfunny smile an unsmiling smile, a 'there are things I can't tell you now son' smile.

Why would he say that? Yes, something was really up. At least he didn't cry. Who wants to see their father cry, the world as you know it end? There he was. Impeccable as ever in his tailored suit, except for that armband. Didn't do anything for him, scruffy thing with some weird sign on it. The really unfortunate thing is this silly armband on the smart suit made me laugh. Of course I wasn't to know it was the last time I would ever see him, but I've had to live with it ever since. The last time I saw my father I laughed at him.

" You can turn the wipers off, Alfons, this switch here."
I reached to the centre of the dashboard and turned
the switch. The blades stopped, the rain so light now we didn't need the swish swish of the wiper motor anymore. Then the car stopped, the rain stopped completely. We stepped out of the Austin, the doors opening backwards, like a black gull.

" Welcome to England, welcome to the Rectory," said the Rev.
I looked around, it was a kind of paradise. Lush trees gently rustling, blossoming late spring flowers, birds singing. In the distance you could still see the smoke rising from the chimneys of the trains entering and leaving the station.
" Leave your belongings there children," said the Rev, " perhaps you'd like a shower after your long train journey."
I looked at him again, the white collar, the honest eyes, the apparent kindness and …yet… the atmosphere of, I don't know, perhaps I am only thinking of the atmosphere now, that word, yes, hindsight. The atmosphere of strain, of gaps between words, of what was never said, the attempt to keep everything at surface level. And who can blame them, who can blame anybody?

There was a peculiar sort of thwack sound, a sound I'd never quite heard before, a violent sound, something being deliberately hit, hard. Thwack, followed by a shout, a boy's voice, just broken , " run" , said the voice, " run."

" Ah", said the Rev, " now you really are in England. Willow on leather, cricket, you know that's how Europe went wrong you know, wars are only ever started by countries that don't play cricket then the countries that do play cricket come in and sort it all out…It's my son and his friends. We have nets in the back garden. You'll meet them soon enough."

Suddenly I didn't feel tired, journey or not, strange people, strange sports or not. If you are curious you don't feel tired. You only become tired when you lose your curiosity. I asked my first questions: " Sir" – don't know why I said sir, seemed to be natural for some reason- " sir, can I play cricket, can I go to the beach, I mean it is a holiday isn't it?"

" Of course , dear boy," said the Rev, smiling, but the smile was like Pater's that last time I saw him. An unfunny smile. Funny how adults always do that. You ask them a question they really don't want to answer and you see that smile. They think you can't see through it but it is really so obvious. Why don't they just tell you things there and then? We always find out, in the next minute, the next month, the next 20 or 30 years. Of course by then you're *completely* messed up.

Then it hit me like a wave, the tiredness, the unanswered questions, the rush to get on the train, the crowds, the sound of breaking glass, of boots running in the street, of neighbours who couldn't meet your eye, parents telling you things that didn't add up.
" I want to know when Mama and Pater will be here," I said to the Rev. " I want to know the truth."

" Ah," said the Rev, " the truth, the search, the truth."

I asked him again. Looking back I think I stamped my foot.

" Alfons," said Sis sharply. " We are guests in this house, these kind people…"

" They will be here," said the Rev, the kindly voice, the gentlemanly voice, disguising nothing.

" When?"

" They will be here," said the Rev.

" When ," I said, " when?"

The Rev looked down. At the grass, the lawn cut into perfect squares.

" Soon."

" When, when, when?"

" One day, one day."

The Rev looked away, back towards the station, the smoke and the chimneys.
.
" You will be with them one day, one day, one day"

 In the near distance, from inside the Rev's house, through the birdsong the telephone began to ring, and ring and ring.

Funny that, telephones can only ring in one way but you know, feel, before you pick the receiver up, you know. A sad call, a happy call, a call that divides your life into two. Your life before you pick up the receiver, your life after you replace it.

The Rev was in the - what did he say in the Austin – the rectory? The windows were open, the English gentleman's tone,

" Good Afternoon. Bridlington 1 9 3 8 ."

Then our eyes met.

Reference: www.hmd.org.uk

CLOSE OF PLAY

The dreams we had as children.

August, another summer slipping away,

Birds high in the sky.

Wickets chalked on the dustbin,

My dad coming home from English Electric;

An over before tea,

Now dinner.

The past, maybe you just grow out of it.

Euro Paean

The PM looked up. " So, how are we –you – going to turn this round? "

The latest opinion poll confirmed what the he already felt. Two – thirds of UK public opinion against joining the Euro.

The Foreign Secretary tried to be diplomatic.

" Prime Minister, perhaps we …"

The PM didn't even look at him.

" I'm not asking you, the politician, I'm asking Francine, our uncommon marketeer. "

Farringdon, the leader from Leeds, was an interesting man, not unfunny, but it was the sort of humour you simply observed, as it went past you, rather than guffawed along with it.

He was " old school ". The " new " stuff was old now. It was back to deals, stitch ups, trade offs, what was possible. In many ways it was a relief; not to have to spin things up any more like a Harvey Nicks window – dresser. Many found Farringdon intimidating. Francine Worth, marketing director, EUBrit, found the challenge stimulating. After turning around Channel Six, a TV station so downmarket it fabricated weather forecasts, persuading Britain to join the Euro would be a cinch.

" Prime Minister, how shall I put this…what do you think about sex? "

" What's our position on this, Foreign Secretary? "

Farringdon didn't bother if the riposte was up to anything.

Francine had his attention.

" Presentation, presentation, pres…"

" Strewth!" exclaimed the PM and HM Secretary of State for Foreign Affairs together.

Francine was holding up an A3 photocopy of latest page 3 lovely Lisa Lone with only two strategically placed ten pound notes keeping the poster this side of the watershed. The slogan underneath the picture read in Sun-style capitals:

CONTROL YOUR INTEREST: YOUR POUND, YOUR ASSETS.

In miniscule print on the edge of the poster there was a short paragraph reading –

" The Euro means your interest rates, your jobs, your economy will be controlled by the barmy bureaucrats from Brussels. Keep the pound, keep control in Britain. Issued by the Vote No campaign. "

" Where the hell did you get that, " said Farringdon.

" I'm taking the sixth " replied Francine. It was her catch phrase from the Channel Six days.

" You're telling us that's the way the noes are going to fight this? "

The Foreign Secretary sounded sceptical.

" I'm absolutely sure. Go as low as you can imagine, then lower, and you might be somewhere near. I'm advising you to rethink your strategy, Prime Minister. "

Farringdon seemed off balance. At a meeting in a Yorkshire Dales hideaway three months ago he had personally committed all their referendum campaign funds to the most ambitious political campaign ever to be fought in British politics. The content was secret, only the methods were discussed. TV advertising, viral marketing, web streamers, endorsements, posters, all explaining why the UK should vote yes and get into the Euro now. The decision was trust the people, education, real information and now they were staring at a tack fest.

The Foreign Secretary visibly reeled at an image of all this state of the art marketing languishing in a Labour party vault in Leeds. The PM heard him saying:

" It would have been helpful if we had known about this before Miss Worth…"

Farringdon couldn't decide which irritated him most; the Foreign Secretary's ability to latch onto the last point but one or the appearance that the opposition had wrong footed him. All his political career Farringdon had made a point of not being nice so he wouldn't finish second. His instinct to take control surfaced fast.

He picked up the red telephone on his desk and curtly addressed his principal private secretary:

" Convene meeting, as before, PM, Foreign Secretary, Chancellor, Press Secretary – and ask the Home Secretary to bring DG MI5. Get with it - now! "

££

Jamie Robertson's Harvard tinged Morningside accent was becoming strained. As leader of the Britain says No campaign his affair with Francine was always highly improbable but nonetheless thrilling for that. Their pact of secrecy and their self administered policy of separating work from pleasure was professionally admirable but personally stressful to maintain.

" No " said Francine, " and as you of all people should know, No means No. It's been a long day. "

" Tell me about it " drawled Jamie.

" I thought we said no more pillow talk. "

" Of course not. But at the end of the day we are a professional couple at the end of the day. Tell me about it... generally. You said no to the non talk stuff so the onus is on you. "

It was late. Francine wanted to sleep. She became unsure of whether she was tired, or tired of Jamie. They had met years ago as rising PR stars. It was all so rock and roll then. Parties, first nights, first editions, feeling you mattered, it was PR people who made policy. A world of oysters and champagne can cloy eventually. She noticed him on her first day at Good Day Knightly. Lying there in bedroom of his Hoxton flat, Francine realised she had never loved him, only admired him. The realisation was so stark it made her jolt. Jamie noticed. Minutes later, Francine, released into clarity, was asleep. Nothing would ever be the same again.

Jamie could intone the economic reasons for not joining the Euro in his sleep – assuming he could get to sleep.

The one size fits all interest rate, the cigars and back slapping of the faceless ones at the European Central Bank in Frankfurt. First the

Euro currency, next Euro tax harmonisation, next...

He felt right in the Britain says No campaign. The he got doubt. How can we accept the single European market and not the concomitant currency, wouldn't it be better to have appointed bankers set an exchange rate rather than leave it to the international speculators? In the evening, talking to Francine, listening to Albinoni, drinking Armagnac, wearing Armani, the doubts came. Maybe it was true, the Britain says No cause *was* about the past. He was sick of references to *the* war, the easy jokes about Brussels. Then the morning came, when he

knew something was different. Francine was going to say No, to him, and he knew why, and why he deserved it.

They never talked much in the mornings anyway. Expresso, tube, text you later.

Jamie did say just one sentence:

" Francine, this Yes stuff, is that what you believe, I mean really? "

" Yes...Yes, I do. "

That's all he needed to know. Francine and Jamie were marketing people. They could sell anything, they knew how it worked, they were the best. Belief wasn't on his agenda. Belief was a complicated option. Francine had got belief. They sat on the tube in silence. At Camden town, the tube split and so did they. Jamie to the No HQ in the City, Francine to the Yes HQ in Westminster.

£££

It was on Highbury roundabout that Jamie lost control. He had stopped taking the tube after losing contact with Francine. It was three days before the referendum. As he steered the Alfa Romeo (he'd buy British after the No vote) into the City lane he saw it.

" WE'RE GOING CONTINENTAL - THE EURO: GET WITH IT! "

screamed the poster. He nearly crashed the car. Slowing down he instantly recognised the famous cricketer and supermodel smiling and brandishing Euros.

Turning into the city road he was stunned again:

The poster was the size of 4 Wonderbra ads combined.

"STUFF THE POUND – THE EURO: GET WITH IT! "

A grey looking man was being refused entry to a club with his pounds. Inside the club you could see wall to wall soap stars, pop - idols, even A-listers, buying the hippest drinks with their Euros.

Jamie struggled to keep on the road. Something had gone wrong horribly wrong. His car phone rang. Jamie answered although his driving at that moment was lethal enough even with both hands on the wheel.

" How's the first day of the campaign going? " smirked Francine.

" Francine…Francine, I told you…You…. You knew…"

" Get with it " she said, " I'm taking the sixth! "

No sooner had he replaced the receiver then the ringtone went again:

The Ode to Joy by Nokia. The morning was spiralling out of control.

Jamie swerved into the right lane as he wrenched the phone from the dashboard.

A white van faced him down.

" Oi, watch yourself mate, get back in the left lane, you think you're doing the continental ? "

It was a marketeer's dream… or nightmare: the posters becoming a street catch phrase on day one of the campaign. Jamie stared at the C3 behind the steering wheel of the van: yesterday he would have been a natural No. The sinking feeling came upon him again. The phone chirped in his ear.

" Jamie, where the hell are you? Get with us. We're losing the war by the minute."

It was Monica, his number two at the No HQ. He noted the ultimate loser's ignominy, your own side loving the opposition's slogan.

In a daze he finally saw one of his own creations – the No poster he was only yesterday so proud of. Times New Roman, no photos, an information poster. The gimmick was it had no gimmicks.

THE EURO HAS NO ECONOMIC ADVANTAGE

THE EURO WILL TAKE OUR SOVEREIGNTY

THE EURO MEANS THE END OF THE BRITISH STATE.

The next thing he knew he was at the HQ in a crisis meeting with Monica.

" You're the Morningside Machiavelli, " she sneered, " get us out of this one. Somehow Farringdon knows what we are doing before we do. Mysteriously all the prime poster sites in main cities were taken in advance. Company called It's Worth It. Bells ring? You assured us Farringdon would bring his campaign so down market he'd be laughed off the sofa. You said…."

" I know what I said. "

Jamie was open about what he said. Only he, so he thought, knew what he had done: sold his soul. He'd deliberately let Francine believe he was going to run the Lisa Lone campaign. He planted the poster on her, knowing she was meeting Farringdon that day. He'd betrayed her. He

was a double loser. The campaign he was already beginning not to care about, it would soon be the past, but there would never be another Francine. He heard Monica continuing:

" We've spent our entire budget. I'm not sure which is worse – the fact that our posters are the deadest ever erected or the fact they are sited where no one can see them. "

Usually Jamie loved Monica's Yorkshire modulation. Today it left him flat.

" But why didn't Farringdon swallow it? How had he realised? He was meant to go for the tack fest. Somehow he'd hit the perfect pitch. I personally…"

he began to say. But even the Morningside Machiavelli couldn't confess to this one.

He'd spent all his capital on a negative, a No campaign. They had lost a vote. He'd lost his way.

££££

It was the day after the referendum. Francine didn't have a hangover, she hadn't stopped drinking Krug all night.

She was ushered into the PM's office overlooking the number 10 garden.

" Francine ! " exclaimed Farringdon. He give her a kiss on both cheeks. " We're going continental. We , you did it ! Two-thirds majority. Champagne ? Just say yes. What now, on to Paris for lunch? You won't even need to change your currency! Or back to Hoxton to Mr No? "

" You knew ? " It was Francine who was off balance - and it wasn't the Krug.

" But how ? "

The PM smiled, " I'm taking the sixth. "

_Fl@me_

From: Richie Montague
To: East Coast Rail, (Lost and Found)
Date: 2 Jan 2008
Subject: BlueBerry

Dear East Coast Rail, (Lost and Found)
Help! My new year got off to a bad start. I've lost my BlueBerry, last consulted on 1430 Kings Cross to York.
My contact details all inside front cover. It isn't the Blue Berry itself that's important. It's the information. No use to anyone else but it's my life in there.
Thanks
R Montague

From: Richie Montague
To: Ms J Catalan Web Designs
Date: 14 February (!) 2008
Subject: Richie Montague

Hey Julia. Googled you. So that's what you do now! Web designer. Fab web site, course it would be, wouldn't it?
How long is it now? 20 years, more? Email wasn't even a glimmer in Bill Gate's eye when it was you and me. Letters then. Kept them all. Can't delete letters.
 No doubt you are as beautiful as ever.
" Age cannot wither her" and all that. Yeah, I know you said I wasn't to contact you again. But 20 years, sentence served.
Why now? Chance of course. Everything is chance. Chance we met, chance we didn't make it.
The point is. I lost my BlueBerry. Day after new year's day. Honest. And no, wasn't even hungover then. Reformed character. Googled every one I ever knew. Found your web site. Broke the silence. Tell me how you are.
 Just a button to press, nothing heavy, don't know where you are @ in real life.
Considering the date I was going to say " your secret admirer" but coyness was never me. I was always a letterman myself, as you of all people know. Moved with the times. I'd have lost you forever if I hadn't lost my BlueBerry and Googled you.
Best wishes, Richie

From: Richie Montague
To: Julia Capalan
Date: 15 Feb 2008
Subject: Long time no hear

Hey Julia. Rich. That web business of yours must be really taking off. I'm a mere click away. Go on, you know you've got time, everyone wants to know what happened to Richie. Exactly why did we go separate ways all those years ago? You and I could have happened together. Evolved. Like any other couple. Maybe we'd have got married have kids. Maybe you did get married have kids? Maybe…look just email me, Julia. Waited twenty years, I can wait two days. Just about.
Very best wishes
Rich

From: Richie
To: Julia
Date: 16 Feb 2008
Subject: You ignoring me or something?

Hey. You're doing it again. Just like you did all those years ago. Old Rich pouring his golden heart out, all I get back is your silence. Heartless hearbreaker.
I'm a dot com millionaire by now, emailing you via telesat from my yacht in Monaco. What do you mean? How do you know that isn't true? Isn't me you say, Rich wouldn't do something like that. OK, I'll tell you something if you tell me something. We both graduated from York University in….well, let's just say before email was invented. I stayed on. You moved on.
I'm still here. You're not. Anyway where are you? Just a word would be well nice.
Love
Rich

From: R
To: J
Date: 17 Feb 2008
Subject: You know what they say…
…about life, don't you Julia? You only come this way once. No dress rehearsal. What happened to us? What happened to you! Can just see you now. Mind's eye. Graduands ball. *That* dress. Strapless. Backless. I expect you are even more beautiful now, if that were possible.
I still love you
R

From: Richard Montague BA Hons (Sociology)
To: University of York Alumni Association.
Date: 18 Feb 2008
Subject: Year of 1978.

1978: Summer graduand ball.
Any photos class mates? Let's get to the point - any photos of Julia Capalan M A . To be more precise, that backless, strapless number. Strictly business.
You all remember Richie " clear the dancefloor" Montague!

Still rockin' after all these years.
Hit the return with those JPEGS '78ers.
Keep the faith,
Richie

From: R
To: J
Date: 19 Feb 2008
Subject: I LOVE YOU

From: R
To: J
Date: 19 Feb 2008
Subject: I LOVE YOU MORE THAN MY RECORD COLLECTION

From: R
To: J
Date: 19 Feb 2008
Subject: I LOVE YOU MORE THAN I EVER DID, YOU'RE SIMPLY IRRESISTIBLE

From: Richard Montague
To: Regency Computer Services
Date: 20 February 2008
Subject: System check ISP
 Could you do a remote check on my email service? I can send but don't seem to receive.
Thank you
R Montague

From: Regency Computer Services
To: Mr R Montague
Date: 21 February 2008
Subject: System Check

We carried out a full check on your system. All clear. If you are not receiving email, whatever the reason it isn't technical.
Invoice in post.

T Bolt
Regency Computer Services engineer

From: Richie
To: Richie
Date: 22 February 2008
Subject: Richie

Hey Richie

Just you and me now Richie, old son. I rang myself up this morning on my mobile so I know it isn't Virgin. Regency checked email system out. All clear. Funny expression that. All clear. May be it's the way I used to dance, clear the dance floor, they used to say, its Rich. Didn't think I was that bad. Flair in flares. Where did all the years go? Email, mobiles, Apples, just new ways of being alone. Loved that girl Julia, thought we had something. I know she never rang, wrote – well just that once to say never write to me again – but I felt it. Always trust your feelings, Rich.
Have to go now, tea to make, toast to pop.
Keep the faith
Rich

From: Richie Montague
To: Julia Capalan
Date: 23 February 2008
Subject: shoulda, shouldn't

Julia
I don't know where you are in the world, I don't care how many years it is. I know back in 1978 I may have overdone it a bit, sending you two love letters in each post every day for two years. Maybe if I'd played hard to get I'd have got you. You shouldn't have smiled at me and if you wanted to turn your back on me you shouldn't have done it in *that* dress. You and I are meant to be. I know your beauty hasn't diminished, my feelings haven't.
I'm not asking for a kiss, just a word. You could be any where in the world, next street, next hemisphere. Maybe my letters were a bit over the top. Now I've kind of found you again, just an email wouldn't hurt.
As ever
R

From: Richie Montague
To: Julia Capalan
Date: 14 February 2009
Subject: I KNOW YOU ARE OUT THERE

Julia
I proved I can keep silent, rational. I mean once a year, hardly excessive.
Tell me something. Let me tell you something: the fire still burns.
I LOVE YOU
R

From: Mr R Montague
To: T Bolt, Regency Computers
Date: 15 February 2009
Subject: I know when to stop

Dear Mr Bolt

Please terminate my email /ISP contract with you with immediate effect. As you put it if I'm not receiving any email the reasons are, well, not technical
Thank you
R Montague
- incidently what does the T stand for? Thunder, Tact, Telling it like it is?

From: Julia Capalan
To :   Richie Montague
Date: 16 February 2009
Subject: As the years go passing by

Richie. You are not going to believe this. YOU ARE NOT GOING TO BELIEVE THIS. Here goes. My son (you read that correctly) was on a East Coast train to York. He's a student there now. (I thank you in advance for thinking I've a son old enough to be a student and I'm *still* so beautiful). Found this BlueBerry. He would have done the right thing eventually -
(that's send it into the lost property office – don't believe everything you read about young people nowadays, besides he's been well brought up) – then recognised your name on it. Yeah, I'd told him all about you. Old Richie, met, as in bumped into, on the dancefloor, took my " it's alright" smile as an invitation to deluge me with more love letters than Laclos. Countless. I mean what's a girl to do? Attention yes, deluging, no. Thought I 'd have a son then tell him when he was grown up in case someone like you ever did it again (JOKE). Did feel a bit sorry for you though. A bit, well… Years go by, I move to LA, set up my own business. Forgot about you. Almost. Sorry. Then this coincidence. Must mean something. I mean tell me how you are, I don't mean hit on me, I mean hit the click.
Best wishes
Julia

From: Julia
To: Richie
Date: 17 Feb 2009
Subject: They're only words
…yeah Richie, two words, I'm sorry. I should have answered your letters, been a bit warmer but you did…all a long time ago now. Water under the…look just reply. We'll take it from there.
Very best wishes
Julia

From: J
To: R
Date: 18 Feb 2009
Subject: Sulk

Hey Rich, come on, sulking is like so 70s. Nothing to prove now. Talk to me. Rich.
" Keep the faith"

Julia

From: J
To: R
Date: 19 Feb 2009
Subject: No more games

We're even now Rich. I was silent when you wrote love letters to me. You are silent to my emails. I'm reaching out to you Rich.
Love
Julia

From: J
To: R
Date: 20 Feb 2009
Subject: I KNOW YOU ARE OUT THERE
Break the silence, heart breaker. I LOVE YOU.
I wish I'd…I wish you'd answer me Richard, answer me NOW.
X

Getting to Yes

" And it is for these reasons I have decided to hold a referendum on the European question once and for all. Let the battle be joined."
Monica had almost turned the news off by the time the announcement came. Watching the news had been part of her evening routine for years now. The news not only kept her informed and connected now she lived alone, it was a link to her unique past. The way she had learned English all those years ago. BBC English her teacher had said proudly. Repeating phrases about war, rape, disasters, so intent on the sound there was no content.

Today it was the other way around. The content overwhelmed her so much. 10 minutes into the bulletin the death toll was already over 1000. The bomb blasts coming closer to home, a civil war in a country with a new name, a flood in the area she had grown up in.

Now the news was at ten, not nine, she carried these images of disaster up the stairs to her bedroom. Images of negativity. There comes a time when you simply don't want to hear the word no anymore. No more negativity, no more reasons why things are not going to work out, for you, or, same thing, for the world.

"Let the battle be joined." The phrase stayed with her. A positive, a yes, all those countries, all that violence between them. She would be involved in the campaign, canvass for yes, no more no.

There was always one street Monica didn't want to go down. You could feel the ' no' streets. What was that expression that was never translated, cul de sac? There was a ' no' street in every area of the city; not just individual houses, the whole street was a no – no.

The word Monica loved to hear, strived to hear, was ' yes'.

Although Monica always participated in elections as a citizen, she never felt inspired to canvass in elections before. Even a poster in her window would be too flamboyant. Bricks had been thrown through windows in previous eras in history, earlier generations had been smashed up, not so long ago. She knew that, felt her connection to it.

Yet there was something about the European referendum campaign that made her want to participate.

In the words of the campaign poster she wanted to ' Get with it.'

The pro EU posters were everywhere now, celebrity endorsements voicing the slogan campaign HQ had devised:

' Let's do the continental: The Euro- get with it.'

Monica rang the local office and volunteered her services. After a couple of hours training – how to close a ' sale', how to cope with rejection, how to ' sell' doubt to antis – she was on the streets.

The thrill of it all. Debating, making your case, seeing a stick in the mud waver. She could finesse a 'maybe' and get to ' yes'.

Monica began to notice her power. She was an unusual canvasser. When Monica first contacted the campaign office saying she wanted to get out there and ' get with it', the response was muted. Why, she thought, isn't the first quality of a canvasser enthusiasm? However, unbeknown to Monica at that stage, the comrades regarded her as a liability. Monica wasn't pretty. She was beautiful, too beautiful. Her enthusiasm was based on idealism not pragmatism, and she still had that Victor comic-style German accent.

Monica had come to England ages ago. It was because of a man of course; an

Englishman, a professional politician. He asked the question, she said ' yes'. Dashing Douglas she called him, with his Austin Healey and his bandits at two o'clock moustache.

He was a MP, a good constituency man, an operator. Oddly enough, at that time she was just like the people she met now on the doorstep who said they had no politics.

How curious that expression was, is. Of course she had issues, but noted they were always opposite to Douglas and suppressed them. Eventually their marriage became a pact, dashing Douglas became dour Douglas with Monica providing the exotic interest. Douglas provided.

He went, eventually, but surprisingly, she stayed. She felt at home, she loved rain, she lived at being different. She added up the number of issues she believed in and joined the corresponding party. Douglas disappeared from her consciousness. In reality they had always been in different parties.

In this campaign she felt she could give something back. The EU was a kind of symbol of the future. She had given up being German, the English could give up being the exception. We'd all be doing the continental.

The days grew longer, the streets meaner. Enthusiasm can only carry you so far. The first weeks were the best. People wanted to hear the arguments, to be persuaded, to argue back. Monica loved the moment the house doors swung open.

Who would be behind it? The Englishmen in their castle, furious at having been dragged away from their tea, thawed quickly, their eyes flickering along her figure in one movement, before returning to her face. The women, suspicious, trying to place her, a competitor, an attention seeker, an agent of change.

The party HQ became pleased with her. The returns from her patch showed the vote was moving. Her innate charm was an asset, she was appropriate in a Euro campaign, she was good at what she did. This referendum was to be held on a constituency basis, they had to win key marginals. Monica was parachuted into Noland, where the resistance was greatest. This week was to be the last push, the message had come through from London, ' Get with it'.

Why was this area, so hard core, so resistant? The research had no easy answers. The streets were mixed in every way: economic background, occupation, education levels. All the categories were represented: yuppies, the grey power vote, ex hippy baby boomers, you name it. Door after door, it was that word, ' no'.

"No, you can't call again," said even the young, single, professional males with only TV dinners as an alternative policy.

" No, my husband isn't in," said the young woman pointedly to Monica as a male voice floated down the stairs, "who is it, darling ?"

"No, but you could help me with my modern languages essay," mumbled a student loser, with the just out of bed haircut.

"No, my mind is closed…"

Monica, trained to be polite, always offered her ' thanks anyway' line as she retreated down the garden paths. She was finding the immoveable noes hard to take. The campaign workers knew the result would be close, but Monica was beginning to think of the doors as a portcullis, there seemed to be no way through.

It was two days before polling day. The focus now was not just on the hard area, but one street. Monica knew immediately. It was a ' no' street. Resolutely she knocked on the first door. Suddenly, she realised she could feel who would be behind the door when it opened.

"I've been expecting you," said Douglas. The smile had no warmth. Of course they had both grown older. Monica had laughter lines round her eyes, whatever had caused the deep lines in his face it wasn't laughter.

" Good morning, I'm campaigning for the yes vote in the Euro referendum, sir, can we count on your vote?" said Monica, not missing a beat.

"Yes," said Douglas.

"What?" She struggled to keep her equilibrium. He was not going to get the better of her after all these years of independence, she was not playing games, she was not going back on his arm.

"Yes," he repeated.

"Thank you for your support then, sir. I'll be on my way." With deliberate dignity Monica walked down the path.

"Yes, but there is a condition."

Monica turned slowly, "what ?"

" I can accept you made a mistake and left me…"

"Left you ? Me ? It was you…you…"

" I can accept you left me, I know what they called me, I know you were always more interesting to the party conferences than I could ever be. But you made a mistake. You joined the amateur party. You could have stayed with the professionals."

"Saying no to everything was never my idea of a profession."

"We know every street in the constituency, we know how to make 'no' streets. We know how to - what shall I say – secure these streets, we know you will lose by 290 votes."

"What do you mean you know how to secure streets?"

"As I said, you joined the amateurs. Your second mistake. I am offering you an opportunity not to make a third."

" What can you offer me? Your whole life has been a mistake. A losing battle with vanity."

"Streets can be secured either way. All you have to do is say ' I made a mistake.' That is what motivates me. I don't care about the outcome of the vote. Idealism was always your department. What are you going to say to me, yes or no?" Monica shivered. In a low, deliberate voice she said "no."
She didn't campaign anymore that day. How can you canvass when you can't speak?

On the day before the poll, street canvassing is not allowed. It was the only point all the parties had said yes to. Monica kept to herself until it was time to go to the count. By now, she didn't hate Douglas, she felt sorry for him.
She realised, again with that shiver, that is what she had always felt about
him. He encapsulated negativity. Their break up all those years ago had seemed without malice, but where had this deviousness come
from? He was almost repellant. She could still hear him pronounce the sentence:
'Streets can be secured either way.'

Douglas had a point. They *were* amateurs, with their clip-art leaflets featuring the typo it was too late and too expensive to correct ('European Parlerment'), possibly idealists, but not manipulators. What had Douglas and his cohorts done? She couldn't imagine. She remembered the no streets, a furtiveness on some doorsteps, a door closing before it had really opened, people mouthing an expression like it wasn't their own: ' No, my mind is closed…'

At 2 am, the second recount began. Monica was beyond sleep. It was after 3 am when the local Constituency Returning Officer gripped the microphone like Rod Stewart about to give a rendition of ' All Shook Up'. Instead, the voice blared out:

"For the No group: 10, 390. For the Yes group: 10, 100."

As the tears welled in her eyes Monica knew it was right to say no to an individual, a representative of the past. Saying no to a negative is a positive.

She didn't watch the news the next night, the extended edition with live feeds featuring champagne-soaked interviewees in the jubilant national No HQ. Asleep long ago, Monica dreamed, of doors opening, of open faces, of people saying to her, in their own voice, ' yes.' The next day she awoke with a smile on her face, a feeling of levity without exactly knowing why.

A week's a long time…

I say
What rotten luck
To cop it a week before the show's over
A poet and all, sensitive soul
Couldn't you see it coming?

I know
Maybe he's simply weary
Move him into the sun,
Worked before,
Bring him round?

Depends
On your point of view
Almost feel like laughing
All they've been through
To cop it a week before the show's over

Mind you,
Could almost laugh at the whole jape
Not the weeks, the years
All over that mud
Can't tell one uniform from the other

Doomed, but
Won't tell a soul
Poets, artists living in a hole
Could almost laugh
Almost

Afterthought
The sun didn't work
This time.

Oxford: in respect of Wilfred Owen

I Loved the Language So Much I Bought It

It was towards the end of his first lesson when Franco realised he was in love with his teacher. She asked him where he was born. No woman had ever asked him that before and listened to his answer so keenly, listened to him as if he was the only man in the world.

' Franco?'

He drifted off momentarily, thinking of the first time he had seen Miriam. She was coming out of her office, with another teacher, who he now knew to be Lucinda. Miriam was saying " I understand your reasons, we all move on sooner or later." Franco couldn't then know the content, the context, but listened to the tone: mellifluous, mellifluous, m…

'Franco!'

' I am being born in Naples,' said Franco.

' No,' said Miriam sternly. ' Again, Franco, please. Think of the tense I am using in my question. Now, where were you born?'

' I was born in Naples.'

' Thank you. Well done. Tenses. So called because they make every one tense. Tomorrow: last day. Social English, for those delicate touches. Now we'll stop for lunch. This afternoon, Veneer at the local art gallery. Meet 2pm.'

' Veneer,' repeated Franco, ' veneer.' He liked to experiment with the sound of new words, the way you had to move the tongue, the lips. This word even felt like it's meaning; smooth with nothing discernable underneath. Just like the English, thought Franco. He'd been here for three weeks now. Franco the English as a Foreign Language Student. Or as his teacher always quipped, the man who puts the F in Foreigner. Everyone he met was so friendly, kind, _nice_. Yet he always felt there must be more.

Three weeks at The Oxford College. Of course it wasn't actually an Oxford College. Franco smiled as he remembered the bright afternoon in Milan, at home, surfing the net, the words Oxford English in the Google search engine. He didn't feel deceived, he had found what he wanted, what he expected. It was the definite article, it taught good English. Oxford English believed Franco. The Principal not only spoke beautifully, she was beautiful.

Franco had seen her photograph on the Internet. Miriam Montford M A (Oxon), Principal of The Oxford College of Contemporary English. Classy touch that thought Franco. Classy, another word he had learned only a few days ago. He loved it. Franco was an exemplary student. Earnest, yes, but what he loved was picking up the vernacular, really getting inside the language. Classy. That was Miriam Montford all over. The portrait Franco had seen on The Oxford College web site was clever. It drew you in. Miriam looked like the business. She'd correct you if you made a mistake, wouldn't fob you off. You felt you could approach her at a social event, of which The Oxford College promised many and much. She looked reachable. Just.

'Hi, Franco, wicked you are here. Cool.' It was Lucinda. Trendy Luce as she was known to the college students. Most of the words she used couldn't be found in any dictionary. And as for her teaching methods…no paper, no books, no right or wrong. 'Pleased to meet you,' replied Franco. He knew as soon as he said it it wasn't right. Stiff. Inappropriate. Of course Lucinda didn't correct him. It wouldn't be cool.

'You look like it.'

She always seemed to be flirting. Franco, often typecast as a " Mediterranean" never flirted back. Not with Lucinda.

'Look like what?'

'Look like you are pleased to see me.'

'What do you want, Lucinda?' Again the tone wasn't quite right. Too curt, aggressive rather than assertive. Perhaps only native speakers could really do that. Of course it merely allowed Lucinda the encouragement to keep on going.

'I love it when you're like that. Are you grooving on the gallery? Always had you down as a sensitive, arty type.'

Franco was enjoying the gallery. It was cool, but not in Lucinda's sense of the word. Cool, thought provoking, centring. He was pleased to be there, but didn't want to spend the time jousting with Lucinda. Her unawareness of her vacuity irritated him. He wanted to spend the time alone with Veneer, perspectives collecting his thoughts, thinking of exactly what he would say to Miriam later when the time was right. How to say the right thing, and how to say it correctly.

Miriam wasn't indifferent to Franco's charm. His linguistic infelicity only added to this. Of course he was rich. A suave, successful businessman. CEO, Globale IT systems, it read on his enrolment form. As Miriam checked her hat in the mirror she checked thoroughly and honestly, that the fact that Franco was wealthy had no impact on her initial attraction for him. It was true. There was a chemistry between them. It was an undeniable wealth-free based truth.

Franco saw her in the ante-gallery, with a group of other students. He didn't interrupt her as the head of the English school explained the Dutch school to a group of Japanese students in English. She caught his eye and held it. He looked away first. Sometimes you don't need words in any language.

It was the last day of the last term. Franco and his class comrades didn't know who would be teaching that day. Of course he hoped it would be Miriam. He analysed honestly why. It was because she was the best teacher, she taught in the way he learned. She had a body of knowledge, she knew how to convey it, she listened. She taught. In burst Trendy Luce. Franco would have to formalise his plan later, just before the final day party.

' Parteee,' announced Luce. ' It's like the last day. Tonight we're gonna party so you need to dress right and you need to speak right. Right? Social English, expressions you will need, let's get real. I'm going to deal you some situations, you're going to match me up some responses. Lets kick off. Franco, you're cornered at a party by the biggest bore in the room. What could you say? Easy does it.'

'What do you mean cornered?' asked Franco.

' Like, trapped, hemmed in, like this,' she demonstrated, standing in front of him. The rest of the students smiled. Franco wasn't amused.

'I'd be saying something liking this: Have you met X ? - find another bore and put them together like this…' He demonstrated, using Lucinda as the stand in bore.

' You're not like insinuating anything now are you, Franco ?'

The chemistry between Franco and Lucinda had never been positive. It was not clear why. Franco remembered some of the idioms he had tried to master from his previous lessons. Frosty. You could cut the atmosphere with a fork. She always seemed to be looking for something from him, he had decided she was the sort of teacher from whom he had nothing to learn. No content. And she wasn't M …
Suddenly the door opened. The frost thawed.

' Afternoon everyone. Thank you Lucinda. I believe you have a farewell party to prepare for. It is traditional for The Principal to take the last lesson of the term. Let's continue where Lucinda left off. Social situations, diplomacy, nuance.'

'Do you mean Lucinda is preparing a farewell party for us or preparing to say farewell to us? Who is leaving whom?'

' Excellent, Franco' replied Miriam. ' I can see the work on prepositions has paid off. As for the party, all will be revealed. Now social situations and diplomacy. Try this. You want to invite a colleague to dinner, but you don't want to appear too forward or …'

' pushy,' interjected Franco, keen to show his mastery of idioms. After all it was the last day.

The party was, thought Franco, a classy affair. So English. The triangular sandwiches, those funny biscuits – crackers. Those improbable combinations; cheese and chalk, no, cheese and pineapple? Everyone in good spirits, the egalitarianism of last days. Miriam arriving in her best hat. So that speeches could be made above the hub-hub a mini PA system had been rigged up by the technical people.

Miriam tapped the mike as if it would burn her. Like many people in her position she thought technology would always go wrong, it would be a barrier to communication, it wasn't neutral. Franco suddenly realised she was going to make a speech. It had always been his plan to speak to her privately before any valedictories. Without thinking he grabbed the microphone first.

' Gentleman and Ladies, I am having your attention please.' He certainly did thought Miriam, realising she was expecting a drama. ' Please look forward to a short rhetoric to be made by Miriam briefly. It is concerning the future of the school.'
After a silence as long as an intake of breath the hub-hub resumed.

' Franco, what is all this? It may be the last day but you are still a student just like all the others.'

' Miriam, I am going to propose to you,' said Franco.

' Franco, this is not the time and place for…'

' I am going to buy the school, Miriam.'

' I've come across some last day pranks in my time but…'

' I am being frank. Here are the figures.'
Miriam knew it was serious. Franco's deals in the European markets had filled many a column in the FT.

' That is certainly generous.'

' There is a condition. Lucinda leaves. The school will teach English the way you speak, Miriam.'

' I am honoured by your financial offer Franco. But I don't accept diktats. And as for Lucinda, her English is as valid as anyone's. You may be able to buy a school, but you can't buy the language. English is a global language. My accent is a dialect, one among all the others worldwide.'

' Your answer please Miriam. Now.'

'You are, Franco, a student like all the others. Now I was making an announcement.'

Miriam tapped the microphone again.

'Ladies and gentlemen. Today we are happy and sad. You come to us as students and leave as friends. And you are not the only ones who are leaving and facing changes and challenges. We are saying farewell to you. We are also saying farewell to our colleague Lucinda…'

In the sea of faces Miriam detected the smile on Franco's lips. She continued, staring pointedly at Franco:

'…who, by an arrangement made at the beginning of our term and by mutual consent, is leaving to take up a position of Principal of the Bondi school of English. We all move on sooner or later. Good on yer Luce,' mimicked Miriam in an appalling, endearing Aussie accent.

' And our final change. We are renaming this school Global to reflect the way English is changing in the world, belonging to no-one, not even our new owner, Mr Franco.'

Her speech was interrupted by a sequence of explosions. The champagne bottles planted around the room by Franco were now being opened in Grand Prix style. Miriam smiled, the speech left uncompleted. She descended into the throng and offered Franco a business style handshake. Franco took her hand and kissed it.

' Champagne and kisses. A revealing cultural response to the conclusion of a business deal,' said Miriam.

Franco held the eye contact.

' That wasn't for my last proposal, my dear Miriam, it is for my next.'

MISSING INACTION

'I miss you.'
What does it mean, where is it located, the missing I mean
I mean you can't miss nothing, can you?
I miss you
If you were here I wouldn't even be thinking about it
Nothing to miss
Nothing
Can't go nowhere there's nowhere to go to
And I'd only miss you there too.
Something only we know, one of our songs
I play the song and miss you to that
Then there's that song by Mick and Keef, Miss *You*, girl
They've obviously been there too.
Where?
That place where I miss you!
That location
That non-event
That everything.
Can't seem to see you anywhere but I see you everywhere all the time.

Then there's that album by Miles
Kinda Blue
As in, I feel blue
Translated for squares means I miss you
But hey, you don't have to be hip to miss people, *the* One.
Miss your hips and lips so.

It could happen to any one
It obviously has-
Therefore all the poems and songs about
Nothing

'Missing in Action'
What 's that supposed to mean?
May as well be dead
So why not come right out and say it
God, I hate euphemisms, wash rooms and all that shit
Why not come right out and say it
'I miss you'
There is something here that isn't.
Right here
In my heart
But if you did an operation, even Christian Barnard couldn't find it there
Because there's something missing so it isn't there.

Sounds like the sort of thing even AJ Ayer would get involved in
Something had to be there so you can miss it when it isn't.
It's a long night without you, star eyes;
Started counting all the stars in the sky
But when I'd finished I still missed you.

And it'll just go on
All night.
A perpetual night
And I'll miss you until there's nothing
And then I'll miss that
And that would be impossible
Because you're everything
And I only wrote this because
I miss you.

Nice Move

Pierre peered through the windscreen wipers.

' This is it. Junction 42. Leeds Centre and North . Our journey ends, our journey begins.'

The Rover careered on.

' Rain,' said Constance ' and, how do they say, chilly. We should have stayed in Nice.'

She played with the pronunciation. ' Nice, nice, Nice, nice. That's all the English ever say. Have a nice cup of tea, what a nice day…'

' It will be as nice here,' cut in Pierre, ' as it was when we came to Yorkshire for our first holiday abroad together. '

One thousand miles due south the conversation mirrored the exchange on Junction 42 but was dappled with Mediterranean sunlight.

' We made the right choice,' said Christine as their Citroen sped along the A8 into Nice. I can see it, feel it, smell it.'

' Yes, the diesel is heavy in the air,' replied Derek with an Aznavouresque shrug.

' If you want to persist with the miserable northerner act that's your affaire,' said Christine. ' smell the lavender, the mimosa.'

' Yeah, I could murder a curry,' Derek came back. ' The thing about French food is an offal myth, and I'm sick of the rude stares all along this death trap auto route I've had to pay for the privilege of driving on and…'

Christine pulled over.

' Right. That's enough. We are here
in Nice, full of sunny opportunities or full of problems. Your glass is half empty of
Tetley's so aptly named Bitter, mine is half full of Cassis. Are you in or are you out?
We both saw the advert.'

They had seen the advert. All four of them, on their respective intranets:
" Unique opportunity – France Telecom and BT job swap. Area Technical Manager
Leeds, Area Technical Manager Nice. 1 year contract following two week
'find your feet' period. Support from local accommodation agent. Don't miss out on
this chance to update your skills – professional and cultural – and experience the good
life in two of the EU's fastest growing cities."

Christine clearly remembered Derek showing her the advert. How he had stressed
the chance to update professional skills while omitting it was also an opportunity to
revisit the scene of their honeymoon, 7 years ago.

Pierre and Constance met the Leeds accommodation agent outside the terraced house.
The agent was managing the house in " Rounday Park borders".
His first words to Constance were ' cheer up love, might never happen.'
Pierre shook hands first, and tried to ignore the way the agent called his wife 'love'.

' All mod cons,' the man went on, 'nice and handy for the Off Licence.
Backyard's sunny as a... Sure you'll fit in nicely.'

Pierre who was so proud of his command of English language and culture began to
falter slightly. However Pierre was encouraged to see Constance warm
to the surroundings. She knew the countryside they remembered was not far away.

In Nice, the agent was now an hour and a half late. Christine had chosen the café for the meeting, just behind the promenade.

At first Christine was in her element, the elegant ladies, the Nivenesque men. Even Derek was making an effort. They ordered two glasses of Gigondas in their best French. The waiter, suave and assured, seemed proud of his profession, unlike the bar staff back home who seemed to take your order as an insult.

' It's really paid off – our refresher course at Leeds Uni,' observed Christine, ' we've had no trouble ordering and these Euros are a cinch.'

' I'll give you that,' said Derek, his gruffness melting by the minute, ' there is one stereotype that seems to be true though, elasticity of time. Must be a lesson there for someone.'

' One might expect some Latin leeway but – what is it now? – nearly two hours is overdoing it.'

As the afternoon continued Christine struggled to reconcile Nice now with the memory of the honeymoon there 7 years back – a time when time didn't matter.

' Madame, monsieur, I'm Chantal, your accommodation executive here.'
Derek stood up, ' Enchanté.'
Christine had never seen Derek stand up to greet any woman anywhere before. It was impossible not to notice the logos on Chantal's dress: the inevitable Hermes, the Chanel sunglasses which stayed on, establishing superiority over the bare eyed Brits. Christine, her forced smile unnoticed, waited for an apology concerning the appointment time. It never came.

For Constance and Pierre things were progressing positively. Over the border in Roundhay the park was green and pleasant. Pierre was pleased with Constance, her efforts to integrate whenever possible, her poise in agreeing to differ if not, the previously undiscovered skill to chat meaninglessly over fences. He had always considered himself a flexible and adaptable man but he noted with concern it was exactly the experiences he had looked forward to in England that were beginning to irk him. At work all was well on the surface but there seemed to be nothing beyond it. He couldn't tell if the famous English humour was funny at all but a way of communicating something which could otherwise never be said. One evening a couple asked Constance and Pierre if they ' fancied an Indian.'

' We'll sample the regional delicacies,' winked Terry, his colleague. In the restaurant Terry drank five pints of a rich, dark beer. His wife seemed to end every sentence with an inverted question – don't you think, wouldn't you, isn't it? She drank nearly as much beer as Terry. Towards the end of the evening she said to Pierre, ' now tell us why you really came here. I mean why should anyone from the south of France want to come here? There is no reason, is there, Terry ?'
Terry asked Constance what she thought of Leeds.

'It seems to have become so continental,' she said. ' the shops, the pavement cafes, direct flights to France too, I mean if we should ever want to go back.'

They never met the couple again socially. Pierre always had this feeling he was at fault. One weekend Constance took Pierre back to the Yorkshire countryside. He never mentioned the past, seemed preoccupied with the future.

' Chantal, I asked you to come here three days ago,' said Christine. She broke into a sweat. She was beginning to hate the agent, who always looked like a Lancome advert. No one can make you feel inferior without your consent, repeated Christine to herself, but she couldn't help giving it to Chantal. Christine itemised what seemed to her easily rectifiable jobs if someone would take responsibility. A tap which never quite turned off, a TV which could only pick up a

cycling channel. The incessant yap from the poodle next door, the drip from the tap had destabilised her. And where was Derek?

At first it was Christine who had blossomed in Nice. She thrilled as she picked fresh flowers every day from the old market. She became a regular at the café off the promenade, reflecting over a citron presse how a woman alone would never feel comfortable in a smokey, darty, pub. Derek's integration was more gradual but total. Occasionally, perhaps late at night with the crickets clicking, they embroidered how good things were ' back home, up north'. Then they laughed. The list of things they missed had become shorter. Christine even forgot that

Derek had forgotten. In 'their' café one evening

they clinked glasses and toasted ' no going back.'

In the ladies Christine reapplied her make up in the mirror. The fabulous art deco frame triggered a memory. This was their honeymoon café. She looked at her reflection then back at the frame. The frame hadn't changed at all.

Derek left for the office early in the morning and returned about 9 pm. No, he didn't want a cooked dinner. Derek's original idea of lunch out, a Wensleydale and pickle roll at the local, was superseded by a three course lunch with *les* colleagues at their adopted local restaurant. He had become so content, so *Mediterranean*. The man who before couldn't bear it if even the slightest thing was wrong with their house now just shrugged his shoulders.

Christine heard Chantal finishing another conditional sentence.

' If it wasn't – how do you say – a Bank Holiday the day after tomorrow I might be able to get the plumber to look at it' and shrugged.

It was the shrug that did it. Christine was at Nice airport within an hour.

It wasn't until she was in the taxi gliding away from arrivals that she

began to think practically. It was the day after the two week ' find your feet' period. Her mobile trilled.

' Christine. It's Constance. I'm obliged to give you a ring after the two week period. Pierre and I are having a big discussion. We went up to the Dales. Stayed in the same hotel we were in on our first trip abroad together.

I am saying we will never go back.

But, Pierre, he wasn't happy here. I said Nice is crazy with crime and cars. He said if he was going to live in a crazy city it may as well be a sunny one. I couldn't make him agree with his own memories. I've decided to stay in Leeds, but Pierre is on his way back to Nice right now! It is not a problem for me, it may be for…'

' Constance,' smiled Christine 'people never move back, they only go home.'

' Chantal, I asked you to come here three days ago,' said Christine. She broke into a sweat. She was beginning to hate the agent, who always looked like a Lancome advert. No one can make you feel inferior without your consent, repeated Christine to herself, but she couldn't help giving it to Chantal. Christine itemised what seemed to her easily rectifiable jobs if someone would take responsibility. A tap which never quite turned off, a TV which could only pick up a

cycling channel. The incessant yap from the poodle next door, the drip from the tap had destabilised her. And where was Derek?

At first it was Christine who had blossomed in Nice. She thrilled as she picked fresh flowers every day from the old market. She became a regular at the café off the promenade, reflecting over a citron presse how a woman alone would never feel comfortable in a smokey, darty, pub. Derek's integration was more gradual but total. Occasionally, perhaps late at night with the crickets clicking, they embroidered how good things were ' back home, up north'. Then they laughed. The list of things they missed had become shorter. Christine even forgot that

Derek had forgotten. In 'their' café one evening

they clinked glasses and toasted ' no going back.'

In the ladies Christine reapplied her make up in the mirror. The fabulous art deco frame triggered a memory. This was their honeymoon café. She looked at her reflection then back at the frame. The frame hadn't changed at all.

Derek left for the office early in the morning and returned about 9 pm. No, he didn't want a cooked dinner. Derek's original idea of lunch out, a Wensleydale and pickle roll at the local, was superseded by a three course lunch with *les* colleagues at their adopted local restaurant. He had become so content, so *Mediterranean*. The man who before couldn't bear it if even the slightest thing was wrong with their house now just shrugged his shoulders.

Christine heard Chantal finishing another conditional sentence.

' If it wasn't – how do you say – a Bank Holiday the day after tomorrow I might be able to get the plumber to look at it' and shrugged.

It was the shrug that did it. Christine was at Nice airport within an hour.

It wasn't until she was in the taxi gliding away from arrivals that she

began to think practically. It was the day after the two week ' find your feet' period.

Her mobile trilled.

' Christine. It's Constance. I'm obliged to give you a ring after the two week period. Pierre and I are having a big discussion. We went up to the Dales. Stayed in the same hotel we were in on our first trip abroad together.

I am saying we will never go back.

But, Pierre, he wasn't happy here. I said Nice is crazy with crime and cars. He said if he was going to live in a crazy city it may as well be a sunny one. I couldn't make him agree with his own memories. I've decided to stay in Leeds, but Pierre is on his way back to Nice right now! It is not a problem for me, it may be for…'

' Constance,' smiled Christine 'people never move back, they only go home.'

Nice University 1976

Remote

Frank hated the way he watched TV. Every Sunday he bought the newspaper. Quality, none of that tabloid rubbish. Many men turned to sports pages first. Others looked at reviews or the health and well – being sections: Dr Ali, Barefoot Doctor, Miriam… He went straight to the TV supplement. Teacher-like, alone, disciplined, he red-penned all his top programmes for the week. He described his tastes as catholic. Documentaries, music, natural history, films made with Arts Council subsidies. It was all quite upmarket, hand –picked, bespoke. After the red penning was complete he felt organised and placed. His week would be fine, no unmanageable chasms. Most evenings began with Channel 4 News. He loved the links : '...thanks Jon Snow on Capitol Hill… now back to the studio in London…' So professional, so structured, like an exclusive club. After that a property programme, maybe with a cultural slant like going to live abroad and never coming back. Or a half hour radio break so he felt he wasn't watching TV all evening then back to the TV. Beating Christ Church all by himself on University Challenge, catching Paxman later with his Newsnight hat securely on. There was a documentary on JFK, a reporter inside Number 10 shadowing the PM during an international crisis.

Weekends? No problem, stay up late (' God, it's 11.35pm'), The Pretenders have reformed for Jools Holland.

Frank loved it. And hated it. Like most addicts he didn't believe he had a problem. How could he? Just think of the golden rules. No daytime TV, no soaps (Heartbeat is a serial drama, set on the Moors he had loved since childhood.). Frank Cleveland didn't have satellite or cable, even though this would eventually cut him off from Test and limited overs cricket. He pretended he hadn't the technical expertise to find the Channel Five tuning. What kind of addict is that? Selection, selection, selection. He thought of his parents in North Yorkshire, the chairs with their wooden arms, arranged around the fire not round the TV. The black and white English Electric behind the corrugated wood doors. The set warmed up exactly before Richard Baker read the news, the fading white spot immediately afterwards. It was the same principle now, even in the modern age. Selection. Don't slip into watching anything, make sure there is a higher ratio of BBC programmes to any other channels.

Frank had other anti-slipping safeguards. He never used a remote control. Two related reasons. He felt the exercise in rising from his chair was part of his anti beer belly campaign and it fitted in with this cardinal principle of selection ensuring there could be no Dante-esque slide into flicking and zapping.

' Addict?' Frank murmured to himself. ' What kind of addict is that ?'

' What do you think you'd miss most about England ?' asked Helen. The way the light shafted into the British Council offices near Trafalgar Square reminded Frank of that painting by Rembrandt, the man sitting by the balcony window, alone, the light streaming in. It was a pleasant memory.

' Mr Cleveland ?' asked Helen again. Frank had almost gone into a reverie. Not a good policy in a British Council interview. Helen Mortaz, Senior Executive Officer for English Language Teaching Recruitment (SEO ELT it read on her work station divider) was a severe looking character. Frank thought he'd shown great discipline in not even giving her black seamed stockings a fleeting glance.

' It's a cliché that British TV is the best in the world, but it may well be true. I don't watch that much TV in quantity but I do appreciate the quality. Especially BBC and Channel 4 news. Maybe I'd miss that most. But then maybe not.'

' Anything else?' searched Helen.

Frank went blank. Beer ? Church architecture ? Oak trees ?

' Maybe you need to go away to be more aware of how you live now,' Frank heard himself saying. He knew he wasn't answering the question exactly. He also knew that organisations like the British Council or VSO recruited people who wanted to go where they were going not get away from where they were. Get away from the consumer, celeb led TV society, get over broken hearts after a dumped relationship. Those getting away rather than going to never went.

' Meaning?' Of course Helen Mortaz pursued it. The interview seemed to have gone well so far. Frank had studied English at Leeds, was widely travelled, EFL diploma from International House, RP accent without being blah. The silence went on. It was the old interview trick. Don't fill your own silences, letting people off at the moment they may reveal themselves.

Frank began what seemed to be a speech.

' Why does anybody want to go abroad? To leave home, to leave the familiar ? How can a person from one country, however qualified and experienced, assume they can go to another person's country and teach them something from their own country? I mean is the Mali Council or the Chad Council sending people here to teach us? I want to go away and teach because I have skills and perspectives that mean I may have something to offer. I assume I may learn something too. I believe in two-way streets.'

Helen stared at him for an age, then nodded, almost imperceptibly.

There was a three-month gap before Frank's cohort of British Council teachers left. First a cooling off period to sort out broken hearts and faint hearts. Then induction and training. On his last evening at home before departure Frank read Africa Confidential and listened to Aida on Opera on 3.

TV ? You can take it or leave it. We've been made to think we need it, it's part of being normal in our society. He remembered a British Council training course he attended a few weeks back. The trainer went round the circle asking participants to say their name and one significant thing about themselves. Of all the introductions he could only recall one . ' Hello, I'm Maddy and I don't have a TV' she'd beamed. It struck Frank as odd, a negative boast. The reaction of the others, especially the younger ones, was also odd. ' Really, wow, what's that like?' or ' you're so brave, so individualistic.'

The British Council area rep roared off along the dust track in her 4 x 4 . The first thing Frank noticed was there were wires everywhere. Villagers were taking electricity directly from crazy looking overhead power lines. 1950s style H shaped aerials stuck out of the huts and houses at all angles. Ingenious satellite dishes were rigged up serving other houses and halls. Wires ran along the street and through the air. There was a constant hum and crackle.

Frank had a wonderful three years. Always working, always outdoors. In the evenings or at weekends he read or walked while the other British Council or Peace Corps types hung around in the TV huts using Camel Lights to bribe villagers to tune into West Wing repeats. Frank was offered the standard one return trip to the UK, air fare paid by the Council, but he never took it. He did have one long weekend up country with Catherine, the earnest doctor from Lille. He met her at the Medecin sans Frontiers Bastille Bash on his first July. They slept under the stars. Actually slept. He rediscovered Pascal and Montaigne with her but couldn't compete with her homesickness. His colleagues invariably described him as calm, centred, professional. He taught well, a good listener, an uncanny ability to blend silence and kindness. Three summers, three rainy seasons, three Christmases. Then the Council offered Frank the customary three-month renewal of contract it gave to all the best diploma level teachers. He never even considered it.

It was a Sunday, three years, three months later Frank passed through arrivals in Heathrow. As a youngish man arriving from Africa he got a third glance by immigration. The bags came off the carousel with an efficiency which pleasantly surprised him. Then he sauntered through into the WH Smith's near the Paddington Express and bought a Sunday broadsheet and a new red biro.

Acknowledgement: BBC radio Ryedale

Smirk

It was always there. Never went away to neutral or progressed into open laughter. Just a smirk. It was there when she when up for the prize.
 'And now at our biannual political award ceremony the award for…'
The TV screen split into four, showing simultaneous close ups of all 4 nominees. An anxious face, an eager face, a surprised face and…a smirk. The screen held all 4 in the frames to see who could show how to lose magnanimously best. Of course Gareth knew it wouldn't be her. He felt slightly annoyed for some reason. How awful it would be to want your partner actually to be the runner up.
 ' …most promising newcomer, from MPs elected at the last general election.'
The presenter feigned difficulty ripping open the envelope.
 ' Davira Hetherington-Turner. Dav.'
Everyone called her Dav. She simply never answered to any other name, didn't even turn round. Even her partner, Gareth, still thought it was a peculiar name. How could anyone come by it? How could it be invented? Did the vicar mess up the lines at the Christening? Was it designed by her parents to give her a head start in standing out? Suppose if she'd been a man it would be Dave. Sort of name rarely fully given: Dave, David, Tim, Timothy…
 Gareth pulled his thoughts back. She reached the rostrum now. The presenter was acting like a rap MC, asking for more applause as soon as the first wave rippled out. ' Let's hear it. Give it up for Dav.'
Truth was Dav wasn't popular. Not unpopular, not disliked, not likeable.
Some people always get their names shortened, some always get an epithet stuck in front. Hardy, plucky, reliable, thorough. Dav got pushy. Pushy fresher, youngest president of the student union, pushed her way to treasurer of the Labour Club. Attracted all the best speakers from British and European Union politics to the University. Dav always introduced them personally. Next day the press coverage was invariable. Dav on the right of the photograph, plus Cabinet Minister, commissioner, chef de cabinet on the left. Just Dav, the big shot and the smirk.
 At the rostrum Dav tapped the microphone. Gareth hated the way people did that. So histrionic, superfluous, a cliché of a reflex like clearing an unphlemged throat. He knew it was just a trick of the trade. That way people were primed to listen to your first word. Without the tap you could be on your fourth word before people listened to the content. Dav tapped, looked up, then around with that same smirk.
 ' Thanks. Great honour to receive this prize, especially from you hard-faced bastards,' she said affably, her arm sweeping across the room full of political journalists who'd elected her to the prize in the first place. ' Everyone should win the best newcomer prize – once.'
She got the laugh she wanted, held the statuette aloft, Oscar –like, for just the right amount of time. Flash cameras went off. She knew what she would look like in the papers the next day. Always did, and always that same bloody …

 'Maybe this will take that smirk off your face,' said the Chancellor the next day with a smile, offering her the most junior of junior ministerial positions in the Treasury. ' Still, greasy pole and all that. Local Government Finance Bill. First Reading. Then get it through both houses and the PM and I will see you right.'
The Bill had graveyard written all over it. Dav, to whom doubt seemed alien, had it on the statute books before you knew it. Pushover. A few well placed telephone calls,

networky dinners, the right fetes in the right constituencies. Plus nowadays the alumni lists of the redbricks could almost match the Oxbridge boys. First Secretaries didn't exactly succumb to the charm – Dav knew her limits – but that expression, that – there is no other word for it – smirk – you couldn't say no.

' The PM will see you now,' said the Number 10 usher. She knew it was a line she would hear one day but even Dav wasn't pushy enough to believe it would happen so quickly. As she entered the room the PM and the Chancellor had their backs turned to her, their gaze fixed outwards across the Number 10 lawn. Only the Chancellor turned and spoke.
' We knew you could do it, Dav. Nice to have that bill on the books. Always did hate local government. Two words that should never be mixed. Local and government.'
Dav smirked as the Chancellor over explained his joke.
The PM spoke for the first time, still not turning, as if Dav was losing in an attention competition with the lawn.
' Fancy a shot at Cabinet level, Dav?'
The door Dav had been leaning against since being a fresher opened so simply.

Next day Gareth opened the broadsheets. The photos showed the PM on the left shaking hands with Dav on the right. Same old pose only this time Dav was with a Prime Minister. Took it in her stride though. In the articles below the photos Gareth again noted those timeworn political expressions- graveyard, poisoned chalice, but he always knew Dav would come through.

In the lead up to the next general election Dav focused mainly on the Overseas Aid (Tazwan Dam) Allocation Bill; the Bill which had seen off the two previous ministers. The government was returned with a slightly increased majority. Dav's face had been a feature of many a screen ad and poster. The week after the election she was still in situ in her office high above St James' Park. The stack of red boxes by and on her desk always at exactly the same height, as she worked through and despatched boxes at the same rate as they came in.

Dav had been a Cabinet Minister for nearly a year now as the evening of the political awards came around again. Late that afternoon the Ministerial limo took her directly to her Pimlico flat, picked up Gareth and onto the TV studios. On the way, as Gareth fixed his best cufflinks he wondered why Dav still bothered with prizes. But she never could refuse invites and the convention was an invite meant a prize. After completing the cufflink operation Gareth was able to give her his full attention. Dav was gazing out of the window, her face just so, the expression that hadn't changed all the time he'd known her. He saw his own face in the rear view mirror. The laughter lines, the Campari at lunchtime lines, then back at her. Smirk lines? Who'd ever heard of them? Of course he didn't want her to lose. After all he had climbed the ladder with her. He enjoyed going up, the accompaniments of such a rise easily outnumbered any downside. So what would the prize be this time? ' Political personality of the year', ' Best cabinet newcomer', ' Most likely PM the election after next…'

Dav swept into the room, a Cabinet Minister now, followed by Gareth and a Principal Private Secretary. Pleasantries were exchanged, contacts restocked. Awards came up, mostly well deserved and graciously accepted, thank you speeches always that right length and tone, two –liners, the self-deprecation of the confident. All the categories except one had been given out when Gareth next looked across at Dav's still unrewarded face. It was shocking to see her. The smirk vanished, the jaw set, the eyes hard and watery at the same time. The presenter dwelt on the autocue. Then the room as one person saw it coming, transfixed by the unwanted inevitably. The envelope was ripped open and the presenter read out the full name embossed on the card inside.

'The prize for most promising newcomer goes to Davira Hetherington-Turner.'

*£urostory / Getting to Yes / **Smirk***

Acknowledgement: Aesthetica Magazine

Soft Machine

Mid life now,

Listening to the first album I ever bought.

Forced to become a teacher 'cos I couldn't play piano like their keyboard player,

You know, the guy who wore sunglasses even in Ronnie's basement at 3 a m.

First girlfriend hated them, only made me like'em even more,

Loved her still, still do,

Even though we broke up before the band did, musical differences.

What was their first (and only) single – 3 minutes, I mean, that's longer than…yeah, yeah right…

Reached 99 in the Melody Maker top 100

Cool, wouldn't want a sell out, I mean would we , man.

Only *I* get it of course.

Time signatures as crazy as the times

13/4   17/8

Johan Strauss I don't think so!

Got F - ed up, Funked up that is, 1978 I think it was

Same as me. We all did. Nothing wrong in that.

Started dancing again in the 90s. Different girl, different time signature – ¾

Dancing classes in the window less hall.

Funny,

Guy there, one of these people you can't make out how old they are.

Waltzes in, dances to his own tune.

Never takes his sunglasses off though, all evening.

Funny that….

In the windowless hall, in the middle of the evening, in the middle of the year, in the

middle of…

Background note:

Soft Machine *formed in the mid 1960s. At first playing catchy single songs their line up and sound went though many changes of style, in particular moving from a vocal sound to a progressive jazz keyboard based sound, merging their live 'songs without words' together often playing for 1 hour plus of unbroken music.*

Squaring the Circle

www.ajr.org.uk

Templeton shouted the signature on my inter rail pass book, a vicar calling 'Well hit, sir,' through a mouth full of honey and tea on the chime of 4.

The feeling I always knew there was something to delayer had led me to divert to this siding, this square.

It occurs to me how much of my life – time space has been about places, squares, yards, quads. Place Saint Sulpice, Radhusplas, Potsdammer Platz. Standing alone - what's new – on the outside of this square I reflect on how these places exist objectively.
I'm either in them or looking at them, a filter. They exist even if I'm not there to see them, or anyone else who was there, in these squares, platz, now, in the immediate past, the deep past, however much of the future is left to me. They'll exist even beyond that, for as long as they really do exist, whether I'm there or not, to filter, interpret. Sort of psuedy fresher stuff you might overhear wafting up from the quad, but takes one to know one.

I look up from my passbook to the sign at the side of me, the Hoch(high) German gothic script reminds me of the sign in that bus station in *Where Eagles Dare* (or some other preposterous *Victor* schmaltz, the banal detail of fiction) .

I double-taked:

'Gasseplatz'

Fair enough. It made me smile, I mean, really, 1938 [check actual date] and all that was so long ago smiling must be the best way to place it this day.

Literally, Gas Square, a Viennese classic, enclosed, grey concrete walls with windows on 4 sides. The side I faced was the way in, a proscenium arch, above it the wall - with the entrance gashed out - and the windows carried on regardless.

I was standing at that point looking in. There wasn't a way out. Particularly if you parked a 6 wheel military lorry there, crammed with rifles, machine guns, stun grenades and other bollocks to stop the residents who might just want to saunter out, go to the shops, post a letter, I mean it was where they lived, the reaction rather extreme, unfair, unsporting, I thought.

The place seemed designed for the event, that event, some twisto architect looked into the future, drew up a minimalist, brutalist (or is that retro?) block of flats around one entrance to be sealed with one lorry.

' Course it bloody upset me, must have upset millions before me, but I could easily move on with my circular ticket, not like all those other poor sods with their cheap day singles which didn't even entitle them to a seat let alone a compartment like the ones I crashed out in on the overnighters. Yes, alright, I confess put my feet on the seats but no-one saw me.

I was 50% into the Inter-rail month.
London, Dunkirk, Arras, Brussels - decent square that – Cologne, Nice, Milan, Innsbruck, Vienna. If Gasseplatz really pissed you off that basically piss off back to Nice, overnighter, step out into the Place of Angels, sun /bikinis /cassis, sod the square, get a load of that trinity.

Stuck. I could hear it all in my head, a lifetime of tinnitus. The clack of shouldered rifles (no, not ceremonial like that parade square behind St James') the stupid thud of boots, the screams of realisation, women, children, men, young old, cripples, morons – you think I'm going to be PC at a time like this – people being sorted out same as I do with my recycling, tins here, foil there, glass here.

Glass. I tracked the windows now, hysterically clean, then they must all have been smashed. (Still clean glass though, like being run over in your best knickers.)

Transfixed at that proscenium there was something further, something not quite placed. That was it, grey everywhere. Grey concrete, grey window frames, even the grey chink of permitted sky above.

Suddenly the symmetry of the closed doors was spoiled. One old lady, ashen hair- must be 80s passed through the door carrying a grey can – didn't even have a proper watering can for Christ's sake! - . She poured the grey water onto the one artefact of colour in the whole place, a pot of geraniums, the red opening with encouragement.

Time. Time to go move. Back , forward, connection to Nice, emerge into the blue, sky, sea, girls, aperitif time: cassis, a life full of life. My white shirt caught the woman's eye. She moved with surprising deftness,
won our game of stare:

' Guten nachmittag, willkommen zum Platz ,'

The sarcasm I learned to survive in the quad came through by reflex –
Can't see what's bloody welcoming about this damn place.

Yet I heard my mouth begin to tell her my name-
Templeton (it must be long after the vicar's tea by now)

'Bitte, what', said the crone.

'Templet….temp….'

She initiated a new game of stare, walk over again. 2 nil. Don't you ever learn? Game over.

146

'My name is Holzelmacher, I said, dredging up the name that had drifted in from the yard to the kitchen in my childhood semi.

'Bitte, what..?'

'Holzelmacher, my name is…'

Again the deft movement, the hand like a sticky windscreen wiper saying , got it as soon as I saw you.

She repeated my name, rinsed it round her mouth, and after what seemed like 50 years, a smile brought red to her cheeks. She must have been quite a catch in her day.

'Wilkommen , ' she said, ' wilkommen, welcome..back..'

The geraniums were coming on nicely.

Squaring the Circle is dedicated to the Hölzelmacher family of Vienna.

Acknowledgement: C Leaver, Skyros 2008

The Greatest Hit
Feat. Junior Wade

Wade was in The Zone.
He loved music. Wade *is* music. He loved music, he loved the blokes in the band, he loved Gloria. That's in inverse order. Gloria wasn't another woman, she was *the* woman, the one who all the songs were about. Wade loved her more than he knew, more than he liked, but facts are facts, the earth goes round the sun, no point messin about.

Doesn't matter how many times you go out there in any gig there is always The Zone. When that's gone you stop.
The band opened with the traditional *homage* ' Crossroads', blasted through ' Gloria on My Mind – wonder what that one's all about – and were well grooving into the second lick of ' Honey and the Jet' when the rhythm guitarist invaded Wade's spot.

'You're in my face, man' said Wade through the monitor backchannel. It's true, the golden oldie about how Junior Wade sacked a bass player mid-riff for this cardinal offence. The keyboard player was paid double that night for improvising on the deep reverb pedal. You never stand in Wade's spot. Never. Don't go there.

There is always a second time.

'We need to get you off stage, man' said the rhythm guitar. ' Platform gantry gonna go.'

Wade glared back, ' you're in my face bro.'

'Close the riff man. Now, off stage left, close the riff, that way there'll be no panic.'

Wade never missed a beat. Glastonbury was the big one. It's not a gig, it's pinnacle city. Next stop heaven. Yeah, some cat droned through the emergency procedures but who listens to that. Ever listened to the flight attendant tell ya where the oxygen is ? - who has that kinda time. Big Guy in the sky has the final word on these things anyway.

The gantry was in Junior's face before the riff was over. That line about ' you see your life flash before you just before the final verse, gig over, no encore, there can only be one way to check it out. (feedback might be a prob but…) it's the same point about accidents – are you lucky because the gantry missed your main neck arterial or a jerk because it crashed on you and not some fourth rate hanger-on bongo basher in the first place?

There is something about the unified silence of a huge crowd, the stillness of terror. Quiet crowds are much quieter than quiet individuals. Wade was on the deck in much less than a second, the left side of his face slashed to the neck. He was down and out. Thank Christ the paramedics were smoother movers than that 60s dinosaur support band.

/
Blood staunched or at least controlled the stretcher was on.
'Sir we need to move you now,' said the lead para.
You gotta give it up for Junior. Wade couldn't stand up, but he'd grown up –

'Damn right boy we need to move, gimme the mike…'

'Sir, I don't advise…'

'Gimme the mike, God damn…'
Junior has spent his whole life (up to now) getting what he asked for, even if this was his last request it wasn't going to be any different. You don't mess with the big man even when he might be about to meet the biggest man of all the other side of the intensive care unit. He could hardly move, spatchcocked, a horizontal martyr, but – praise the lord – the wound seemed shut at last. Some neck.

'Listen up folks,' – the charm of Junior's north London southern Louisiana drawl was unaffected. The crowd turned with one face, like a flock of emigrating birds.
- 'Listen up, folks, I don't know if it's my time, I ain't afraid to meet the Good Lord time of his choosing – bit if it is or if it ain't I ..I …gotta say one word to y'all: '

Wade was woozy, black in a pool of red, grounded, everyone wanted to give the statue a plinth, would he go before the one word was transmitted?

'Folks, I wanna tell ya…one word…Gloria. You gotta love your woman, above all, anything, worship her, stay close'
The image swam into him, the black of her hair, the dewdrop sweat (couldn't the woman stop being elegant for once!) on the black brows as she gave him young Marty. Their first born, the beauty, the honour of her black triangle, the image pulling him forward to the mike for one more surge –
'You gotta…Gloria…Gloria,' sister morphine beginning her sweet riff, rippling through Junior Wade, the ultimate music…Glori…Glor…Gl…'

Unrequited

Swarming. That's how it seemed. Not sweet bees but wasps, hornets. That's how it seemed to Terence. Malevolent. Everything against him. Photocopier. Water cooler, office managers desk. All swarming with busy people. Director of studies, students, teachers. Terence couldn't get to anything. Anything he wanted. Photocopier to prepare 20 copies of an exercise on which his professional life depended. Water cooler to assuage a thirst induced by a hangover so aggressive he decided to give up trying to cure it and just go straight into the next, and of course, Helen, the office managers desk, and behind it , Helen, managing. Managing of course because unlike Terence she didn't have to work with unrequited love. That's how it seemed. To Terence.

Unrequited. Terence thought of the word. If he wasn't thinking of Helen, he was thinking of words about or for her. Sexy? Too direct, common even, as in " you men are all the same, only want one thing". Charming? Not sexual enough. Not specific enough. Physical charms or charming manners? Useful word though. One of those words you can actually say out loud to women, see how they react and decide more specifically, what, if anything it's worth trying next. Yes, unrequited. Not ambiguous like charming, not one track Neanderthal like sexy, but tragic, Bryonesque, hopeless, spurned. Unrequited love, a one way boulevard.

Amongst the swarm Terence drifted into a reverie. Byron? Tennyson!
" For words like Nature, half reveal
And half conceal the Soul within."

"I hold it true , whatever befall
I feel it when I sorrow most
'tis better to have loved and lost
Than never to have loved at all."

Poets, words. Of course he wanted Helen the way men he would consider crude want women but he, offered more. Words. Nothing flash. A car you could take the lid off, a house on a taxless shore. Words were what Terence did. Put words in his language into the heads o f people who already had a language but needed another. That's where he came in, he had inside him the words they wanted inside them. But couldn't get to the photocopier to put the words on paper to transfer them. Byron may have had his own obstacles but at least he didn't have to put up with this photocopier shi….

' Leave those with me, I 'll see to them for you.' said Helen, gliding from behind her desk to in front of him in one movement. Helen always glided never walked, glided. Terence checked himself mouthing a 'who me?', there was no one behind him of course, there was Helen in front of him. Between him and the swarm.
At the critical moment the words failed him.

' Er …well….perhaps….' Hardly Byronesque. Lost for words in front of the only prize he ever wanted to win.
' Chin up, stiff upper lip, best foot forward.' Terence still hadn't moved, like an animal in headlights instinctively equating stillness with invincibility. Helen's feet moved just one step forward. Closer. 'Here, I'll do them in the break.'
' But what about, how am I going to get to the break without…'
'First lesson, improvise. Off the cuff, up your sleeve, don't get hot under the collar…'

Helen smiled at him, magic smile. The word that always went before her smile was magic. She took the work sheet from him and glided away. Terence was all alone in the classroom, no Helen, no paper, just words in his head.

The first formal (as opposed to social) lesson was always tenses. Logical, if you think about it. *If* you can think about it. Past Present Future. Mistakes, lessons, hindsight, possibilities. All to play for, everything in front of you. Terence looked out. 20 faces looked back at him. He felt like a concert pianist, brilliant at playing from sheet music but you take the manuscript away and…nothing. The thoughts came before the words. But who had taken the manuscript away? Helen. She had obviously noticed enough to help him. In at the deep end, sink or swim, help can come in many guises.

The words came to Terence silently first –

' Time present and time past
Are both perhaps present in time future,
And time future contained in time past.
If all time is eternally present
All time is unredeemable.
What might have been is an abstraction
Remaining a perpetual possibility
Only in a world of speculation.
What might have been and what has been
Point to one end, which is always present.
Footfalls echo in the memory
Down the passage we did not take
Towards the door we never opened…'

Poetry, again Terence said to himself, poetry, and what the hell use is that? My kingdom for a photocopier.

' Tell us your life story' he said to Franco in the front row ' Biography, tell us the truth, o r how you would have liked it to be.'

There is always one. Terence wouldn't normally use a self- appointed clown on principle but that was only a principle on paper. Perhaps it was the forward beak of his baseball cap that pushed Terence. Emblazoned on the front were the words "Yale Athletic", though Franco was decidely neither.

' I am being born in Naples. I am living by the Cathedral. I am loving…'
Terence made a high eyebrow open palm gesture, wordless but universal.
Arabella took it up.
' I am being born, I think not, I was born, I think so.' Teacher Terence accepted the input with a half smile, funny how mistakes can be so much sexier than being right, he thought apropos…

' Thank you, Arabella. Right. Yes, Franco was born in Naples. He lives by the Cathedral. And he loves…' he hesitated for a quarter of a second, love, did he want to go there, then he remembered he had no paper, the only material was… ' who do you love Franco?'

Franco's hesitation wouldn't even register on an atomic clock.
' Helen, I am loving Helen.'
' You mean I love Helen,' Terence heard himself saying, the inflection neutral.

Terence got through to the break somehow. Amazing what you can do when you have to.

Break. Interesting word that, reflected Terence, switching off the lights as he left the classroom. Break, suggesting destruction rather than a rest, or something violent between two periods of creation. No time now to pursue thoughts of words. Action. He sought out Helen with even more alacrity than usual.

' You saved my life,' he said with a controlled smile that dimpled his cheeks rather than bared his teeth. Control he didn't feel but if he " lost it " in front of Helen he would lose everything. She wouldn't be at all impressed.
'Yeah I know,' Helen's smile was flawless, but must have floored many a man, must have, Terence believed. Radiant. Captivating, magic. Making everything alright, turning rain to sun. The only cloud that flitted across the sky was Franco. A rival. A student. He dismissed it. Had to. That way sanity lies.

' So', said Terence, arms unfolded to receive the documents. ' As I said you saved my…'
' I know.' That smile again. Giaconda.
' And how can I thank you?'
' I haven't done anything. I gave your sheets away. Well, one of them the rest I …'
' You….'
'You don't need them. Hanging on to something. You have everything you need.'
'But…'
' Here take this.' Helen gave him a single sheet of white photocopier paper, folded in half.

Terence slept even less than usual. He folded and unfolded the paper endlessly, blank except for the single letter I typed just above the centre of the fold. Now it was so late he got up early, even before the first chorus of birds. He forced Helen out of his mind to plan the second lesson. It was important for a teacher to make a good impression at the beginning of a course, rather like wearing Armani on the first day, then any old cheapo cast off after that. You're still Armani man for the whole term. You never have a second chance to make a first impression.

Swarming. Again. Conspiracy. Obviously a secret competition on, who could get in earliest and SNAFU Terence at the photocopier. But before you could even say 'Alfred Lord' Helen glided in. Something in the way she moves. Effortless but unaffected, not catwalk at all.
'Give those to me' she said, 'I'll sort it.' Terence did what she asked, handing over his prepared worksheets, and minutes later was naked, paperless, in front of the class.
He realised he hadn't given out to the class a single sheet of paper. The class looked at him, the second morning, that sea of faces facing him, all their folders pristine. Franco in the second row, the peak of his baseball cap turned sideways. Terence saw his file was open. He read the title page upside down: " Tenses." Their eyes met.

Terence made sure Franco lost the staring competition. You have to show these people who is boss, early. Then Terence looked out into the sea.

' Today. Prepositions. Arabella describe your room. Sentences. Please.'
By now Terence reckoned he'd clocked the different types in the class and how to co-opt them. Jokers, nerds, derailers, detail freaks, perfectionists, leerers, sulkers, pets.
Arabella was the class pioneer. There's always one, you can use to pathfind the others. Arabella began dutifully underlining the prepositions with an invisible marker pen.
' I live <u>on</u> the first floor, if you look out of my window you can see <u>across</u> the street <u>into</u> the park. My desk is <u>by</u> the mirror. If you go up the stairs you come to the …'
Terence smiled and cut in,
' Thank you, Arabella. Continue Franco.'
Franco held Terence's eyes again, then slowly transferred his gaze to the open file and began to read:
' There is too much sex and violence <u>on</u> TV nowadays. Some people have written <u>to</u> the producers of TV programmes to complain. What is the world coming <u>to</u>? The producers invariably write back that each generation complains about the last, that complaints show that people are being challenged <u>by</u> the programmes. The emphasis that Franco *seemed* to place on certain words irked Terence. Sex, complain, challenge. Then this thought was almost instantly dispelled. How had his lesson got into Franco's file?

Terence was uncharacteristically direct to Helen. I t was early the next morning after another sleepless Helen filled night.
'What happens to the work sheets I give you to photocopy?' he asked her.
Helen simply put her finger over her full lips in a 'shhh' gesture and silently took his next set of notes from him, cover page: modals. Just before she turned to leave she passed him another sheet of white paper, almost pristine accept for the capital letters YOU typed just under the fold.
She took her hand from her lips and placed it against his temple. It was the first time she had touched him.

153

' You have everything you need in here. You must believe.' And she was gone.

Terence stared at the class staring back at him. His mouth opened: ' today's lesson is…'
' Modals', exclaimed Franco, in the third row, baseball cap back to front, his exposed forehead emphasising the gauntlet of eye contact.
' Do we *have to*', said Arabella, coy smile.
'Nice one, Arabella' and found himself smiling, relaxing. Without thinking he put the palm of his hand to his temple.
'We don't *have to,* Arabella, but I think we ought. Now, everyone, work with a partner, examples of something you should do, ought to do, have to do, but never can, could or may and consequences. 10 minutes each way.'
Time flies when you're having fun, the break arrived before he even wanted it.

There was no swarm round the photocopier the next day. Terence merely smiled. He had nothing to copy.
Helen appeared from nowhere, everywhere.
'There's something in my office you may want' she said. Terence was normally irritated by people who appeared from nowhere, but Helen was Helen. He simply marvelled at her effortless glide preceded simply by the slightest swishing sound. Her sound.
'After you, ' he said, his arm sweeping and spiralling with the apparent gallantry of a court poet. He followed her into the office, eyes firmly on her, a split second before he knew she would look round he brought his eyes up again, professional, neutral.
In her in tray 3 sets of class material – tenses, prepositions, modals, each set flagged 1 – 19.

' I thank you', said Terence transferring his gaze from the copies back to her eyes, 'but …'
'That's right, you don't need them anymore, you have all you need here.'
Again that gesture to the temple. 'Well, maybe you do need what is on this paper.'
The sheet was folded with four letters directly in the middle. Helen smiled magically.
Terence opened it, blushed , just slightly, then his smile joined hers.
'See you in the break'.

Untitled by Anon

'I miss you.'
What does it mean, where is it located, the missing I mean-
I mean you can't miss nothing, can you?
I miss you.
If you were here I wouldn't even be thinking about it-
Nothing to miss.
Nothing
Can't go nowhere there's nowhere to go to
And I'd only miss you there too.
'Something only we know', one of our songs
I play the song and miss you to that.
Then there's that song by Mick and Keef, Miss *You*, girl
They've obviously been there too.
Where?
No Where?
That location
That non-event
That everything.
Can't seem to see you anywhere but I see you everywhere all the time.

Remember that album by Miles
Kinda Blue
As in, I feel blue
Translated for squares means I miss you.
But hey, you don't have to be hip to miss people, *the* One.
Miss your hips and lips so.

It could happen to any one
It obviously has-
Therefore all the poems and songs about
Nothing

'Missing in Action'
What's that supposed to mean?
May as well be dead
So why not come right out and say it
God, I hate euphemisms, wash rooms and all that shit.
Come right out and say it
'I miss you'
There is something here that isn't.
Right here
In my heart
But if you did an operation, even Christian Barnard couldn't find it there

Because there's something missing so it isn't there.

Sounds like the sort of thing even AJ Ayer would get involved in
Something had to be there so you can miss it when it isn't.
It's a long night without you, star eyes;
Started counting all the stars in the sky
But when I'd finished I still missed you
So started on the black holes too.

And it'll just go on
All night.
A perpetual night
And I'll miss you until there's nothing
And then I'll miss that
And that would be impossible
Because you're everything
And I only wrote this because
I miss you.
YouFemIsm.

Up and down

The spiral staircase was such a downer. Lancing trudged up. 16, 17, 18, 20 same as his age.
At the top he had to shoulder open the stuck door .
The room made his heart skip a beat – this was what it all led up to – then it sank. Oxford , city of lost causes, the college a 14th century ecclesiastical foundation, always had the noun prestigious dumped in front of it. Lancing had no time for prestige, a concept, a waste of time. Prestige is something old that doesn't work properly.

'The journey of a thousand miles begins with a single step.'
He dragged himself into the gloom of his single room. The bed, a monk bed, shouted at him, lost cause, double would be a waste of space. Like Lancing himself he thought, thoughts spiralling out of control regardless of any assertive techniques they'd filled him up with at the crammer.

Lancing drew back the curtains, the reflex of moving in to a hotel room. To his credit he smiled : behind the curtains was a picture of the college, not bad actually, a water colour signed by some fellow, depicting the quad in May , a scene of open panes and window boxes.

' Yeah, hard brie and all that, bloody door is a bastard too. Still expect you 'll hardly be in here, ' said the tall figure, flashing a smile, not a wink at the bed.
Lancing turned. The figure seemed to have glided in, the door no issue for him, the A in b*a*stard lasting a century. A hand unravelled from beyond the double-cuffs–

'Terence Honeymann-Scott'

'Lancing'

'Zillion syllables, I know, let's just leave it as Tez. I'm across the way, room mates. Calls for a snifter before dinner, join us, drinks, dinner, post-prandial cruise over to Charlie's for an Armanac or 4.'

Lancing followed Tez across the landing. Immediately in Tez's room he drank in the view.
Oriel window wide open, dappled evening light, fragrance from the flowers on the sills, beyond The House bell's.
Tez hovered over the Vermouth long enough to register Lancing's reaction to the view, the discrepancy between the two rooms.

'You haven't got to take these issues personally, Lancing,' said Tez, 'it's just the way things are.'

Lancing's reflection on the usage of his own name in comparison with Honeymann-Scott's sexy self-allocated nickname was smoothly interrupted by the chime of the Cathedral bell.

Dinner slid down Tez's throat. Lancing checked his companion's shiny black Oxford's for castors as they proceeded along the High to Charlie's college.

It was Charlie who moved forward to shake hands with Lancing, her hands so fabulous even the finest silk gloves would only make them seem rough. As he raised his eyes from her hand to her eyes she kept hold of his hand, an eternity of a millisecond. He never checked the view from the window in her room, didn't seem polite or relevant. Looking back he never checked any other view again.

'Charlotte, Charlie to you, so you are Tez's room mate, Lance – er…?'
'Well, across the landing actually but..'
'Mmm how divine, wish this college had gone co-ed, mind you , a landing between Tez and I would just be a waste of space!'

He never felt three to be a crowd though he did turn down the 5th Armanac.

Lancing came down with a borderline 2:2
Over the second sherry in his exit tutorial the don inquired why he'd ' taken his eye off the ball' just before finals. Lancing almost gazed out of the window.

The alumni web site chronicled Charlie and Tez for a couple of years. A cricket blue for him, the effortless first then a radar blip when Lancing - if he thought of it at all – had this image (no, it wasn't even the first Armanac) of Tez moored in a clipper of some sainted Carib island, Barts, Lucia, Kitts…They weren't exactly the waters Lancing sailed in. Charlie? Radar isn't designed for silhouettes like that.

Lancing worked, tubed, bed-sitted – didn't take it personally, that's just the way things are.
His institute, one of the slightly less fashionable think tanks, wasn't the smartest of places. Deep in NW1, his office door clanked against the filing cabinet, like a shutter in the mistral. Not exactly Nobel calibre nonetheless Lancing's econometrics made ripples, a refereed journal there, invitation to feed into shadow cabinets there…

The new colleague was rumoured to be pretty hot stuff, although her field was the subject of speculation at the institute's water coolers. It was just another May morning when the Director of the Institute blew in to present the new appointment – he actually had to stand behind Lancing's door as he introduced her.
That hand – more used to be kissed than shaken - was outstretched .
The director's voice curved round the door, 'I have the pleasure of introducing our new colleague Charlotte Hetherton, this is....' – he faltered realising he'd never known Lancing's first name, come to that he'd never seen him smile but he'd put that down to the econometrics and..

Charlotte graced in

'Lancing, Charlie, I'll be just across the hall from you.'
Her hand continued its journey towards him, like those arms that snug onto aircraft doors, the touch simply a reconnection from where they took off.
She spoke first:
'Nice view,' her eyes still on his,
Lancing smiled: 'It's just the way things have always been.'

(Acknowledgement: M Roffey, Skyros 2008)

2 x Winters Tales

1 The first student of the new year

The building was as cold as the student. Taciturn Norwegian (*Taciturn* Norwegian as opposed to what?!). Same age as me , same sex , same continent but he has cold eyes, white beard. I don't.
Stay open John I said to myself. It's your job to stay open. We walked into the room.
'Hello, I'm John . I look forward to working with you this week. I've been a trainer for York Europe for 10 years'
How would he react? Pleased to have a trainer with that experience *or* someone stuck, scared, unable to imagine how to move on?
His reaction was no reaction.
I talked more, pleasantries not banalities.
No reaction.
Hours, days, no reaction. I tried everything I knew, I even tried things I didn't know.
No reaction.
Two can play at that game. I waited and waited until some thing was given back to me from the cold man in the cold room from the cold country. Finally he spoke:
" John, let me tell you about forbidden love."
Blimey I thought. And he talked and talked in a kind of flood.
How he met a woman at his work while he was in another relationship and she wasn't.
How when he became free she was in another relationship. He lived alone in a bohemian part of Oslo.(his word -bohemian. Sounded cool. Perhaps in estate agent-ese bohemian is code for something different?)). Spacious airy flat. He wouldn't move, literally from this flat. He wouldn't express his love to someone who wasn't free, who was in another relationship. So he talked of forbidden love.
I listened.
Of course then he asked me about myself. I said it was beyond me sphere of competence. The Norwegian said ' you're a man' I opined 'You can express love in different ways. Moving in with people is just social convention. And….
That may be so he said. But where are **you** going?
Where are any of us going? It's a journey not an arrival, I said. Anyway tell me what happened in the end?
He resumed his story: When we were both free, we moved in together. I waited and acted and gave something up and got something back. I lost to win. I fear for you John he said, you will stay still and you will lose, you will *miss*.
On Friday I left the room while he talked to my boss about the week.
How was your week, said the boss, 25 years experience of open questions.
John is a good teacher , the student said to my boss, me out of the room. And a good man.
No, What about your week, said the boss, the director of the company.

We both learned, the Norwegian said. Later I read the form he left on the desk, upside down. He'd gave me a " 5 ". The highest mark possible. I wonder what the high 5 was for.
I wonder what happened to him. I wonder what happened to me.
Then the Spring came.

Winters Tale 1

Winters Tales 2

2 Thames Bloke

Westminster Bridge, scene from Monet (or was it Renoir?). I worked in the office until 4. It was New Year Eve, 1980 something. Don't know exactly when. Wham ! were in the charts if that helps to place it. London. A single man. Time when possibilities so infinite you could end up doing nothing. New Year Eve. So what! Dates are just numbers.
31.12.198-
Train home and unwrapped dinner, scanned the paper. Caught a bus to the river. Flurry of snow.
Went into the pub, that pub by the river, Putney, you know, Oxford v Cambridge. Bought a pint, saw her.
" I think I could fall in love with you," I said. I never have had chat up lines. It wasn't the pint talking. Hadn't even touched the froth , but I said it anyway.
" Thank you," she said. A dark beauty, white teeth appeared in her smile against her black hair. " Join us, if you are alone."
I was so I did.
The midnight kiss lasted a year. Then she left, gave me her address. She mouthed the word at me: Write. I was on one side of the bridge she on another.
I wrote.
And wrote and wrote. Became a professional letter box checker. George (or is it Paul ?) singing Please Please Mr Postman.
Years.
I found someone else, but I always wondered. I hate " what ifs", they stop you sleeping. The new relationship was great. Lasted three years before it began to go wrong. Three years. Not sure if that is a success or a failure. I knew it was going wrong. But I fought to save it, be loyal, talk, walk, sort of bloke I am.
John there is someone to see you said the other person who lived in the same flat. Richmond.
Went downstairs, It was her, girl I said I could fall in love with. The feeling was still there. Feelings can stay the same for millions of years, like nuclear material buried under the sea.
We went out. Sorry I didn't write she said. I'm free now. I'm not I said, loyal still to a dying relationship but how was I to know.
I'll wait she said. I just want to hold your hand now.
Time passed. She even took me to a night club in London once, not far from the river. But we were never free again at the same time. What's that unpronounceable album by The Police called: Synchronicity….something like that.
Had a Christmas card from her last year. Couldn't make out the postmark…somewhere On Thames maybe?
Me. I'm in a different city now, different river.
" My son and I send you our love".

No mention of a bloke except of course her son, he's a bloke if you think about it. No mention of any bloke, but there must have been, I mean I know it was Christmas but the Immaculate Conception only happened once as far as I'm aware.
Wasn't me, could have been though, could have been…
Putney, Hammersmith, Richmond, Chelsea. Westminster Bridge, all those bridges, all that water flowing under….
Still think about it you know, the 4 AM what if…

Winters Tales

j

Your Rubbish

Stayed up 75% of the night hearing your save the planet pitch.
In the morning found all 9 of your San Miguel bottles in the bin, the one clearly marked non recyclable.
Heard you'd flown to the Maldives to chill out. Heard you tell me you'd carbon traded but I know the trees you planted would only take you as far as Antwerp. Unshredded paper bank statement in same bin as the bottles. Yeah, you're a cheapskate too.
Upsets me. You never offset. All your hot air, your sophomore words less substantial than a descending vapour trail. I hope the sea levels rise on your beach, wash your shorts away, those £90 a leg Vilebrequins sweated up in some dump the wrong side of Hanoi.

Heard you'd left it all behind but all you left was all the lights on. You said it keeps the criminals out but you're one too. Planet murderer. Heard you explain you can turn satellite boxes off standby without losing your presets but found you crashed out in front of MTV honeyz with the sound on mute. I mean what do you care about 'cept you?

Heard you boast you'd taken the Land Cruiser back to the dealer, lectured the guy without a tie that you couldn't justify it any longer, then heard you spent the afternoon burning up the bypass bypass courtesy of the dude's S class talking torque. Can't think what the S stands for, or why someone like you is in a car called ' class' at all.

Heard you'd given up burgers , so why's the Whoppa wrapper in the bin next to the San Miguels? You 're so rubbish you can't even make a choice about the right bin. And no, I don't have to explain what I was doing in the bin anyway. No, YOU get a life. Exactly what is your point? Yeah, I heard what you said. I said I heard you.
Planet'll be bloody toast before you listen.

WISE GUY…
And other fables

INDEX:

WISE GUY

P4 – 83	
+	
84 - 88	4 x4
90	As If
91 – 97	Before and After Now
98	Close of Play
99- 107	Euro Paean
108- 113	Flamed@dot.con
114 -121	Getting to Yes
122	Long time, a week
123 – 127	Love the Language
128	Missing in Action
129 – 135	Nice Move
136 - 138	Remote
139 – 141	Smirk

142 – 143	Soft Machine
144 – 147	Squaring the Circle
148 – 149	The Greatest Hit
150 - 154	Unrequited
155 - 156	Untitled by Anon (*or* Quite an Ado about Nothing)
157 - 159	Up and Down
160 - 163	Winters Tales, 2
164	Your Rubbish

ISBN 978-0-9558519-0-2/York European Publishing

J F T King © 2009

www.johnkingcommunications.co.uk

Acknowledgements

Aesthetica Magazine

Amerland Enterprises

Elsie & Terence Fagan

Stephanie Hale,   University of Oxford

Guy Morgan,   University of York

Alan Ram,   University of Leeds

Monique Roffey, Claire Leaver,   Skyros 2008

Katharine Sands   UCLA

…

Author photograph: AH/ (also on *Facebook*)

www.ingramcontent.com/pod-product-compliance
Ingram Content Group UK Ltd.
Pitfield, Milton Keynes, MK11 3LW, UK
UKHW021320180426
11947UKWH00015B/1344